The Other Place

Scott Nagele

The Other Place

ISBN 979-8-9864071-0-4

Polar Squirrel Press
Okemos, Michigan
U.S.A.

First Edition 2023

For Mom

Her art lives on.

About the Author

Scott Nagele grew up in the Mohawk Valley of New York State. He currently lives in Michigan with his wife and three sons. His other books are *Temp: Life in the Stagnant Lane*, *A Housefly in Autumn*, and the story collection, *A Smile Through a Tear*. He also writes a humor blog, "Snoozing on the Sofa" about fatherhood issues.

Scott can be reached at: scott.nagele@yahoo.com

Find out more about Scott Nagele's books at:
www.scottnagele.com

Read Scott Nagele's fatherhood blog at:
www.snoozing**on**the**sofa**.com

ACKNOWLEDGMENTS:

Without the help of generous people, this manuscript would never have been published. I owe a great debt of gratitude to several people: In chronological order, I'd like to thank Paul Nagele and Tom Woolsey for their willingness to read and give valuable feedback. Thanks to my editor, Val Mathews for pointing out the sorts of things an author can't see in his own work. Special thanks to Ana Carlson, for her effects on the cover and to Meg Elias, Jayme Taylor, and Ann Johnson for combing through the proofs. As always, I must give enormous thanks to my wife, LaRay, for her constant support and encouragement, and to my boys for always making sure I don't concentrate too hard on any one particular thing.

The Other Place

The following is a work of fiction.
It is inspired by true events.

Chapter 1.

Emma twisted her fork in her mashed potatoes the way a child does when she is thinking with them rather than eating them. "Daddy, when will we go to the other place?"

Rob swallowed his food. "What? You mean Pennsylvania? We'll probably go there this summer when we can swim in the lake."

Emma shook her head. "No. I'm not talking about Aunt Clara's. I mean the *other* place."

Rob glanced across the dinner table toward his wife, Marcia. He shrugged his shoulders at her before turning his gaze back to Emma. "I don't know which other place you're talking about, if it's not Pennsylvania."

Emma had been watching her fork turn in the mashed potatoes as they talked. Now she lifted her attention to her father. "You know. The *other* place."

Marcia took a turn with her daughter. "You mean kindergarten, honey? You'll go there next fall, after you're done with preschool."

Emma breathed a long sigh. "That's not what I'm talking about either. I'm talking about the other place. The. Other. Place."

Marcia's eyes met her husband's puzzled expression. They made inquisitive faces at each other.

"Do you know what it's called?" Rob asked.

"No," Emma replied.

"Have you ever gone there before?" Marcia asked.

"Well"—Emma widened the tunnel in her potatoes and squinted her eyes—"sometimes I dream about it, and then sometimes when I wake up, I'm not really sure it was a dream at all."

Rob smiled and nodded. "Ah, a dream world. Now I get it. Do you enjoy going there?"

Emma pursed her lips and held her fork still. "No. I don't think it's very fun. Daddy, what's a duty?"

"A duty?"

"Yeah. I think that's what he called it."

"Well, a duty is something you have to do because it's what you're supposed to."

"Like brushing your teeth?"

"Yes. Like brushing your teeth, or telling the truth, or doing your chores."

Marcia cut in. "Honey, you said that's what *he* called it. Who's *he*?"

"The Gatekeeper."

"The who?"

"Gatekeeper. He's the one that takes you to the other place."

Marcia put down her fork and did something even Emma knew you weren't supposed to do. She put both elbows on the table. She leaned forward on her elbows and asked, "How do you get to the other place?"

"There's a door in the stairs."

"What stairs?"

Emma tilted her head just a little. "The ones that go up to our bedrooms."

"You mean our stairs? The ones in this house?"

"Yeah."

Marcia rolled back off her elbows and picked up her fork again. She allowed herself to send a little smile across the room toward her husband.

Rob returned his wife's smile and then turned it toward Emma. "Well," he said in a jolly voice. "I didn't know anything about that. We'll certainly have to take a look at it after dinner."

"Can't," Emma corrected him. "It's only there when it's dark and everybody is sleeping. That's when the Gatekeeper comes out and makes the door be there."

2

"Well, I'd like to take a look just the same. You don't mind if I look, do you?"

Emma began filling in the hole in her potatoes. "No."

When the dishes were all put away, Emma found her dad tapping on the wall under the stairs with his knuckles. "Well, it seems pretty solid to me," he said with a wink as he saw her come nearby. "There don't seem to be any breaks in the wallpaper either."

Emma shook her head. "That's not where the door is."

"Oh? It's not?" He made a show of scratching his chin. "Where else would you put a door on this thing?"

"I'll show you." She walked to the foot of the stairs and pointed at the steps about a third of the way up. "That's where the door is. The stairs open up, a whole bunch of them. And there's other stairs that go down to the other place."

"Oh. Well, let's see." Rob walked up the stairs to where she had pointed and rocked on the step. "I don't know. It seems pretty solid to me. Are you sure this wasn't all just a dream?"

"Daddy, I already told you it was a dream." She smiled with the words, realizing he was just being silly with her.

"Oh yeah. I guess you did. Don't I look foolish, looking for dream doors in the stairs."

Emma's smile faded. "At least, I'm pretty sure it was a dream."

Rob came down the stairs and put his hand on Emma's head. "I'm pretty sure it was, too."

Chapter 2

Tucking Emma into bed, Rob asked her if she thought she would dream about going to that place through the door in their stairs.

"I don't think so," she said. "I only dream about it once in a while."

Marcia kissed Emma on the forehead. "Are they bad dreams?"

Emma thought. "No, not really bad dreams."

"Are they good ones?"

"No. Not good either. It's always kind of cloudy there and cold. I like sunshiny places much better."

"Well," Marcia said, "I hope you dream about a sunshiny place tonight."

As the parents walked downstairs together, Marcia grabbed Rob's arm. "Oh my God, she had me going for a minute there!"

Rob smiled. "You don't like your daughter talking about her visits to mysterious places?"

"My Lord! I was about to yank her out of preschool, with all this talk about other places and gatekeepers. You don't know the horrible thoughts that flashed through my mind before I was sure it was all just in her head."

"Yeah, I do. They were flashing through mine, too. Do they have a janitor's closet at that school?"

"I don't know, but I was about to find out." Marcia let out a deep sigh. "I'm so glad she told us it was all a dream before I went down there and made a fool of myself."

"We were about to become crazy, ugly parents, weren't we?"

Marcia became pensive. "It sounds like she's had this dream more than once."

"That's how she made it seem."

4

"You think that's normal?"

"I guess. I mean, it's hard to remember that age, but I feel like I probably had a recurring dream or two. At least, a recurring theme to my dreams."

"Yeah. I guess so. It's just that I worry about her sometimes. I mean she's so perceptive for her age. I think back to when I was that age. There was a boy who was leaps and bounds ahead of the rest of us—mentally, I mean. He seemed like a miniature adult to us. But then he started acting weird. He just got weirder and weirder, until one day he wasn't in our school anymore. I don't want her to be like that."

Rob laid a hand on each of Marcia's shoulders.

"She's not like that. Yes, she's a bright kid, but she's not quite ready for Harvard. She'll probably be on the high end of her kindergarten class next year, alongside two or three other bright kids. And I bet none of them will act so weird they need to be taken out of school. Being on the bright side does not make you a weirdo. Neither does having a few strange dreams."

"You're right. I know you're right, but I just can't forget about that one little boy."

Rob smiled at her. "That's your problem. You went to school with smart kids. You should have gone to my school. We were all dumb. We were as weird as we could be and nobody batted an eye. They just said we didn't know enough to act right."

"How'd you end up so smart, then?"

"My wife and daughter are always teaching me all kinds of awesome stuff."

"That's sweet. A little sappy, but sweet. And I know I probably worry about Emma too much, but it's always the bright kids who get overwhelmed by things in their own minds. She said some things that made me wonder if she isn't already beginning to struggle with the line between dreams and reality."

"I think she knows all that 'other place' stuff was just a dream."

"I hope so, but there was a moment when I wasn't sure. And for life to make any sense, there's got to be a firm line between dreams and reality."

Chapter 3

Emma climbed into her car seat and strapped herself in.

"Can you get it, or do you need me to help you?" her mom asked.

"I don't need any help. I did it all by myself," Emma assured her.

Marcia started the car. "I knew you could. You're getting so big. You hardly need my help with anything anymore."

"Just wait until I get to kindergarten. Then I'll be able to do everything."

"I don't doubt it," Marcia said into the rear-view mirror. "But let's worry about having another good day at preschool first, okay?"

"Okay, but let's hurry. I don't want to be late. There's an extra $20 in it for you if you step on it." Emma got that one from her dad. He'd heard it in a movie and he liked to say it when he needed them to hurry up.

"Yes, ma'am," Emma's cabbie replied.

As they wound their way toward the school, mother and daughter concerned themselves with their own thoughts. The only sound in the car was the soft hum of the tires turning on the road.

Marcia drove mechanically the route she had taken so many times in the past year, allowing her mind to wander to the list of errands she would complete while Emma was in school. There would be lots of things to talk about after school, but the drive to school was the time they could both use to anticipate how their days would go.

Emma started to sing softly to herself. She was fond of music and did this frequently. Marcia often hummed along to the tune. Emma never began a song Marcia didn't know—not until today. Marcia couldn't identify this song, so she listened harder. The melody was foreign to her. She concentrated on trying to catch the soft words.

> *"Yesterday, upon the stair,*
> *I met a man who wasn't there.*
> *He wasn't there again today,*
> *I wish, I wish he'd go away..."*

Marcia knit her brow and looked into the mirror. "Emma, I don't know that song. Is that one you learned in preschool?"

"No. It's not a school song."

"Did Daddy teach you?"

"No."

"Where did you learn that one?"

"I don't know. Just from myself, I guess."

"You didn't hear it somewhere?"

"I did hear it somewhere, Mommy."

"Where?"

"I heard it one time when I went with the Gatekeeper."

"The who?"

"The Gatekeeper."

Memory widened Marcia's eyes. "Is he the one you told me and Daddy about, a couple of weeks ago? The one who has a door in the stairs?"

"Yup. That's the one."

"Did you dream about him again?"

"Yeah. I mean, I think I did."

"Did he take you to that place he takes you?"

"Yup. He did."

"And you learned that song in your dream?"

"Yeah. The Gatekeeper sang it when we were making braids in the cows' tails."

"What cows were those?"

"There's this barn where we go, and we were braiding the cows' tails. I don't know why. The Gatekeeper thought it was funny, so maybe that's why."

Marcia stopped at a red light and looked back around her seat at her daughter. "Does he make you go to that place, Emma?"

"No. I go on my own."

"Do you like going there?"

"Not really."

"Then, why do you go?"

"Mom, the light's green."

Marcia faced front and accelerated. "Why do you go?"

"Because it's my duty."

"Who said so?"

"The Gatekeeper."

Marcia pulled into the school lot. As Emma hurried out of her seat belt, Marcia came around to hug her. "Does this Gatekeeper scare you?"

Emma shrugged. "I don't know. A little bit, maybe. Not too much."

"You let me know if these dreams get too scary, okay?"

"Mom, I'm gonna be late."

Marcia walked her to the door and let her go. If it didn't scare Emma that much then she would try not to let it bother her. She set her mind on that as the correct answer and went about her errands.

Chapter 4

His presence made her open her eyes. It was dark, but she knew he was there. She could feel him standing beside her bed. It startled her, but after a second, she knew it was him and she was not afraid.

She didn't enjoy it when he came to her like this. She didn't like getting up out of her warm bed to go with him to that snowy place. Yet, he did not hurt her, and she knew, somewhere deep within her sleeping mind, it was only a dream. Pleasant dreams were best, but at least he hadn't brought her nightmares. That was something to be grateful for, and being a grateful sort of child, she obeyed him in her dreams.

"Good evening, Mary Ellen," he said when he was sure she recognized his presence.

"My name's Emma."

His voice matched his condescending smile. "Yes. Of course," he agreed, but a child is the perfect one to understand when a grown-up is humoring her foolish ideas.

"Do I have to go with you tonight?" she asked.

"That's why I came here. You see that, don't you?"

"Yes. Of course," she said, trying to give his condescending tone right back to him.

He didn't seem to notice. "Very well, then. Shall we?"

Emma rose from the bed and put on her robe and slippers. Together, they left her room and walked down the stairs. Though he intended her to go where he wished, he made no attempt to take her hand or spirit her along by physical force.

At the bottom of the stairs they stopped and silently turned around to face the steps. She was sure he did something to make the next fantastic event happen, but she could not discover what it was.

Whether it was a blink of his eyes or a silent word from his lips, she could never tell. Whatever his secret command, the crack in the stairs became visible. It was a squared U, beginning eight or nine steps up, running down to the third step, cutting across the width of the steps and turning back up to end at the opposite side of the step where it began.

An odd kind of light shone through this widening crack. It was a light without any glow to it. It was not bright, but it lit things in a twilight, grayish sort of way. It allowed one to see, but it showed a world of outlines, without illuminating the details of anything. If darkness could shine, this would be the effect of its rays.

The stairs within the U of light rose, pivoting upon some unseen hinge that connected them to the upper stairs. The lines of light widened and converged upon each other until they created a square opening large enough for an adult to duck through. Nothing could be seen through the opening except the light, which seemed quite opaque in its dullness.

The gray light illuminated the Gatekeeper in its gloaming way. He was a petite man, certainly shorter and slimmer than Emma's dad. He wore a plain, dark suit of old-fashioned clothes. The triangle of his shirt that showed under his jacket was white, but even it seemed to dance with dark shadows. His shirt's collar was pulled together by a thin, ribbon-like bow tie of black material. In his hand, he held a felt hat with a brim all the way around it. He always carried his hat when he was inside.

He extended his hand toward Emma without touching her. "After you."

Emma stood still. "Are you sure I have to go?"

"Oh yes. Quite sure."

"Because it's my duty?"

He nodded. "You've learned it well, Mary Ellen."

Emma conquered her reluctance. She put her head down and walked through the opening, but not without chiding her guide. "Emma!"

She didn't know how this wide-open country could be located underneath the stairs in her house, but she supposed things like this were allowed to happen in dreams. Even so, she always looked behind her, first thing, to see if she could look back into her house. She never could. Behind her was the same snowy and windblown landscape that lay ahead. Above her were not steps, but only a monolithic layer of gray clouds.

The ground was flat and open, with only a random tree here and there. On the horizon spread a distant wood. The tall grass, though bent by wind and winter, stood out in tan, dead clumps above the snow. Behind and to the sides, the ground rose gently until it turned into forest, which met the sky at some indeterminate place in the distance. Ahead, the land sloped down toward a cluster of wooden buildings.

The cold hung all around Emma, but it did not bite. Something reassured her it was more annoying than dangerous. Though dressed only in pajamas, robe, and slippers, she did not fear. It was as if the cold were only a prop to add credence to the dream.

The snow was the most prominent feature of the landscape, yet when Emma walked through it, it did not stick to her slippers, nor did it melt against her exposed ankles. This too was for effect. She knew when she awoke, her feet would not be wet. But she could not wake until it was time, and so she must walk through pretend snow and feel the chill for a while longer.

Emma knew they would walk until they arrived at the buildings. This is what they had done every time before. She only wondered why the doorway to this land was so far away from their destination. It was a long walk, and it seemed like things should require less exertion in one's dreams.

She recognized the buildings; she had been there before. They were a modest house and an equally modest barn, with a little shed and something that might have been an outhouse nearby. She knew what kind of things the Gatekeeper would have her do when they got to the farm, but she didn't know why he would have her do them. It all seemed rather silly, but that's what you get with dreams. Things don't have to make any sense at all.

She might have asked him why they continued to do these foolish things on their nocturnal visits to this strange place, but she kept silent. Something told her that if she asked a dream question, she would get a dream answer. That kind of answer wouldn't be worth the effort of asking. Besides, she preferred it when he didn't talk to her. There was something about his voice she didn't like. This made perfect sense, since there was nothing else about him she liked either. He, and his foolish trips to the country, occupied her mind when she might have been dreaming about having a pony. Even if he hadn't been so weird, that alone would have made him unsavory.

At last, they came near the buildings. There was nobody around. Though it seemed to be the middle of the day, lights cast their glow through the windows of the house, making it look like the residents therein were preparing for the onset of evening. It added gloom to the outdoors.

The barn was not very big, but it looked like it was tilted a little to one side. Because of this, Emma didn't like going into the barn. She feared the short side would give way and the entire structure would collapse down upon her. Nonetheless, she entered the barn when the Gatekeeper motioned for her to do so. He followed her in. Even when entering a barn, he took off his hat.

It was even darker inside the barn than outside. It took a moment for Emma's eyes to adjust, but she knew what was there. To the left, hay was piled against the wall. To the right were three stalls. In the first stall was a mule. A cow occupied each of the other two. The mule was lying down. He raised his head to look at them as they entered. They did not interest him, so he put his head back down.

Emma expected the Gatekeeper would instruct her to set the cows free. That's what he made her do last time. She didn't know why he wanted the cows set free. It didn't seem like a very nice thing, going around letting loose people's livestock. But then, if the people who lived here weren't real, then it didn't matter anyway. It kept the Gatekeeper tolerable, or as tolerable as Emma figured a creepy guy like him could be. Besides, she supposed it didn't really hurt anybody.

This time, the man did not tell her to untie the cows. That was not the only difference. From the third stall came a new sound. Emma could not identify it, but it didn't seem like any noise she had heard cows make before. She peered around the corner of the third stall and immediately jumped backward.

The third stall housed its cow, but there was also a person there. This was a shock to Emma, as they had never encountered people in this place before. They had always done their mischief and left, without ever knowing if anybody besides animals lived here.

The person was a girl, older than Emma, with long, dark hair. She was sitting on a wooden stool beside the cow, working at its udder to squirt streams of milk into the bucket below. Emma wanted to take another peek at her, but she was afraid. Even at the quick glance she'd taken of the girl, Emma felt disquieted by her.

The Gatekeeper, noting Emma's shock at seeing another person, smiled at her. His smile held no warmth, only a hint of disdain. As an example to Emma, he boldly stepped to the back of the third stall, in plain view of anyone inside. He planted himself upon firm feet squarely across the exit of the stall. Staring down at the happenings within the stall, his smile turned to a quiet laugh. He glanced at Emma and shook his head, with its self-indulgent grin, at her. His laughter grew in volume.

Emma anticipated a shriek from the girl in the stall as the Gatekeeper made his presence unavoidable, but no human sound came from there. All Emma could hear was his laughter as it grew disproportionately loud relative to anything she found funny within this barn.

Just when it seemed his mirth would go on forever, he fell silent, as if nothing had ever been funny. Emma had never seen somebody laugh so hard and then not laugh at all in the space of an instant. It added to her dislike of him.

He motioned with his fingers for her to come near. She peeked around the corner of the stall again. The girl was still sitting upon her stool, attending the cow as though no one had been laughing the most uproarious laugh at her.

"Come," he said to Emma. "She can neither see nor hear you."

"Is she deaf?" Emma asked.

"Only to us," he replied.

Emma stepped into full view of the girl, who kept at her work. The sound Emma had heard from the stall was the milk splashing into a pail as the girl coaxed it out of the cow with her fingers.

The cow turned its head over its shoulder and looked back at them. It let out a little snort that, from a human, might have indicated a certain level of disgust.

The girl looked up from her work. She glanced around the open end of the stall, looking to see if there were some tangible cause for the cow's actions. Satisfied the cow had not been disturbed by anything earthly, the girl patted its side and spoke soothingly. "What's the matter, Fanny? There's no one here but me."

The cow stared past her to where Emma and the Gatekeeper stood. She shook her head from side to side, as if flies were bothering her, but this was winter.

"It's all right, Fanny," the girl said. "I'm almost done anyway."

Emma leaned toward the Gatekeeper, ignoring how unpleasant it was to move nearer to him, and whispered. "Why can't she see us?"

15

"Why do you whisper, child?" the Gatekeeper answered in a booming voice. "Speak up, if you please!"

"Why can't she see us?" Emma repeated in a slightly louder voice.

He chuckled. "Because, my dear, that would break all the rules. We must have rules. That's why you're here after all, because we have rules."

"Who is she?" Emma asked.

As he spoke to Emma, the Gatekeeper seemed to take pleasure in watching the girl at her milking. This last question brought his eyes back to Emma. "You don't know? You don't recognize her?" He shook his head just a tiny bit. "Why, Mary Ellen, that's you."

Emma's lips fell apart as her eyes widened. "No. No."

The Gatekeeper smiled. "Of course it is. Take a good look."

Emma was already taking a good look. For one thing the girl was much older than she was. The girl was almost a grown up. She did have the same color hair and eyes as Emma, and her complexion was similar. Her nose even had the same shape to it, but she was far too old. And you couldn't be two people at once.

Emma shook her head violently. "Maybe her name is Mary Ellen. I don't know about that. But my name is Emma, so she isn't me."

He moved near the milking girl. "Very well. Watch this. Take care to watch her eyes." He touched the girl on the ear. She swung her head toward him, alarm written on her face. She rubbed her ear as she searched all around for the cause of the sudden sensation.

"Did you see?" he asked Emma. "Did you see the look on her face? It's the exact same look that was on yours when I told you who she was."

"She can feel it when you touch her?" Emma asked.

"When I wish her to," he replied. "Watch. It's as simple as wanting her to feel my touch." He brushed the girl's cheek with his fingers. Her hand flew to her face so fast that he barely had time to remove his own. Again, she searched all around, and even above her head, in case a spider dangled down from above.

"Fanny, do you see any flies in here?" the girl asked the cow. The cow blinked her eye and chewed her cud. "No, there can't be flies now. It's too cold. And it wasn't your tail that touched me. I've felt your tail against my face, and it doesn't feel like that."

The Gatekeeper watched all this, silently giggling to himself. "You see," he told Emma, "I can make her feel whatever I want."

Emma frowned. "It doesn't seem like a very nice trick to play on somebody."

"My, but aren't you a fuddy-duddy for the little sapling of a person that you are? It's all in good fun. There's no harm in it. Here"—he pointed to Emma's hand—"why don't you give it a try? You can make her feel you, too. Just pat her on the head, why don't you?"

"No. It's a mean thing to do." Yet, it was tempting. It was a rare power to be able to stand right in front of someone and not have them see you. It was amazing, and more amazing still was the idea that you could touch them and decide if they would feel it.

The Gatekeeper ignored Emma's words and read her eyes. "Oh, go ahead," he told her. "How many times do you get a chance like this? You spend the nighttime being afraid of Boogey Men. This is your chance to be a Boogey Man. You don't get to do that every day, do you?"

Well, if she just touched the girl very lightly, Emma supposed it would do no harm. She would only do it once, just to see what it felt like. She stepped next to the girl and raised her hand over the girl's head. Emma had to wonder if Boogey Men ever got scared, because she felt nervous. Her hand trembled as she lowered it. She tried to be gentle, but at the very instant her hand came to rest upon the girl's hair, the cow turned its head to look back over its shoulder at her and let out a low bellow.

This was too much for the milking girl. She leapt to her feet, knocking over the stool and sending the startled Emma hopping backward. The girl had run halfway out of the barn when she stopped short. She turned and looked back at the pail of milk on the floor beneath the cow, thinking better of leaving the product of her labor behind. She gritted her teeth and charged, head down, back to the cow and retrieved the pail. Resuming her flight, she spilled large splashes of milk at every step.

Emma looked down at her own body. Though she had jumped backward with a start, she had not moved out of the panicked girl's way. There could be no doubt that the girl had actually run through Emma in her eagerness to escape. Emma touched her own chest. It felt as solid as ever. The Gatekeeper stood to the side, grinning at her.

"She went right through me!" Emma gasped. "How did she do that?"

He shook his head a little. "It has to do with time and space, and a lot of other things that I won't waste time on. It's far too much for your five-year-old intellect, Mary Ellen."

Emma's face reddened. She could tell he was belittling her, and she didn't like it. "I bet you don't know, either," she mumbled. She ached to tell him he was just a mean, old man, who wasn't nearly as smart as he pretended to be. Yet, behind all her dislike for him, a growing fear of him hindered the free expression of her thoughts.

The Gatekeeper's face grew serious. "We've wasted enough time playing. Now, it's time to get down to business. Come here, child." He moved to the pile of hay.

The gravity of his tone told Emma that she should swallow her anger and obey. She went to his side, searching his face all the while, attempting to predict whether his next expression would be a smile or a scowl.

He reached into his pocket and extracted a small box. He opened the box and took from it a matchstick, handing both the match and the box to Emma. "You know what to do."

Emma shook her head and quailed from taking the items. "No. I don't know."

He gave an exasperated look. "Surely, you haven't forgotten your favorite hobby, Mary Ellen."

Emma gave him only a blank stare.

He looked upward and shook his head with vigor. "Children!" he muttered. Grasping Emma by the wrist, he forced the box into her hand. He pushed the match between the fingers of her other hand. "Enough of your childish games. Strike the Lucifer on the box!"

Emma's lips quivered. He had never used this angry tone with her before. Nor had he physically coerced her like this. She slid the head of the match against the side of the box. There was no chance of this creating fire, so timid were her actions.

"With a little gusto, now!" the Gatekeeper scolded. "Do it like you mean to make a flame!"

Emma tried again. Her fingers trembled; the match nearly flew from her hand. This swipe caused less friction than the last.

"Don't play with me, child!" He swung around behind Emma and took control of her hands with his own. He squeezed her fingers tightly around the match. With a quick stroke, he guided it along the side of the box. The match burst into flame. "There now. That's better. It's all coming back to you now, isn't it? Of course it is. There's no firebug the likes of Mary Ellen MacDonald."

Emma ignored his using the wrong name for her again. She was transfixed by the burning match in her hand. She'd never been in charge of fire before. There was something exhilarating about it.

"Now, touch it to the hay. Quick, before it goes out!"

The thrill was gone. Emma's hand resumed shaking. "I'm not supposed to play with matches."

19

The Gatekeeper threw back his head and let out a loud guffaw. "Ha! That's rich, Mary Ellen! Ha! You? Not supposed to play with matches? Who told you such foolishness?"

"My parents."

"Your parents! What would they know about it? I'm the only one who knows what you are supposed to do, and I say light the hay."

The match burned down close to Emma's fingers. Though she did not wish to start a fire, her instincts made her drop it. It extinguished itself before it hit the hay.

The Gatekeeper growled through his teeth and snatched the box from Emma. He opened it and took out another match. "Here, now. Let's try that again. And don't waste so much time. Just do what I tell you this time."

Emma balled up her hand into a fist when he tried to force the match into it. "No! I don't want to start a fire! I don't want to be a bad girl!"

The Gatekeeper reached the end of his patience. He pried Emma's fingers open. "Take it, damn you! I tell you, it's your duty!"

"No! It's not! It's naughty!"

He bent over, took Emma by both arms, and thrust his face down toward hers. "Listen! Do you want your parents to be hurt? Do you want something horrible to happen to them?"

Emma fought back tears and shook her head.

"The only way you can protect them is to do your duty. Now strike the Lucifer."

A tear ran down Emma's cheek, but she had stopped shaking her head. The Gatekeeper let go of her arms, leaving red marks where he had squeezed.

Emma struck the match, this time with enough determination to produce a flame.

He stood back with his arms folded. "Now, the hay."

Emma sobbed as she touched the match to the top strands of hay. She expected the pile to burst into flame, but it did not. Some of the strands took the flame reluctantly. Others only allowed themselves to be singed. When the match burned down, Emma dropped it. Both the hay and the match extinguished themselves.

"Too damp!" He spit the words out the side of his mouth. Searching about for better tinder, his eyes settled on the contents of the partial loft above him.

In the loft were stacked bales of straw. The Gatekeeper climbed part way up the ladder, reaching for the nearest bale. He pulled loose some straw from the side of the bale, twisting it all up together into a makeshift faggot.

Climbing down to the floor, he made a little hole in the pile of hay with his hands. He commanded Emma to strike another match, which she did without trouble. Once the match was lit, he took the box from her hand and replaced it with the straw he had bundled. She knew what he intended, but she waited until he ordered her to light the straw.

Once the straw caught, he took hold of Emma's hand and guided it so that she was pointing the straw downward, allowing the flame to grow up its fuel. Emma would have dropped it from fear of the flame, but he made her hold it until he was satisfied with the size of the flame. Then, he let go of her hand and nodded toward the hole he had formed in the hay.

Emma let her torch fall into the hole. This time the hay could not resist the flame. It burned, though not so eagerly as the straw did.

The Gatekeeper nodded a single nod. "Good. It's all coming back to you now, Mary Ellen. Now we can go." He turned to lead the way from the barn.

Emma stood still. "What about the cows and the donkey? I don't want them to burn up."

He beckoned her from the doorway. "They are not my concern. Come."

"No. I won't let them burn!" Emma started toward one of the cows to untie her as she had done on previous occasions.

21

She had gone but two steps before his hand caught her by the arm and pulled her toward the exit. "Would you rather burn up yourself, foolish child?"

The hay was not good fuel and the fire burned slowly. Emma was confident she could release all three animals without danger, but the Gatekeeper's pull was too strong. "Let me go! I can save them!" she cried, but she was dragged into the open.

Emma's excitement was subdued by a new sight. A man, wearing suspenders over his dingy white shirt, emerged from the house. His dark pants and leather shoes looked old, and so did he. He didn't walk like an old man, but his thin, scraggly hair and his beard made him seem so.

Emma and the Gatekeeper watched the man come to the barn. As he walked around to the doorway, he saw the fire within. Then he moved with the energy of a young man. He picked up a shovel from against the wall and began beating down the flames. Owing to the vigor with which he worked and the modest volume of the flames, he soon had the fire extinguished. He looked about him to assure himself that there was no more danger.

At last, he stormed off toward the house, yelling, "Mary Ellen! Get out here!"

The Gatekeeper sighed. "It was very damp hay, after all," he said to no one in particular.

"Is he going to yell at that girl for starting the fire?" Emma asked.

The Gatekeeper huffed at the question. "Why, I would hope he'd do more than yell at her. It's very dangerous to start fires in barns. If she doesn't know that by now, perhaps she ought to have a much sterner punishment."

"But she didn't start the fire!" Emma protested.

The man puckered his lips at her. "Well of course she did. She was the only one in the barn at the time. Who else would have started it? The cow?"

"We started it."

22

"We? Now, don't go dragging me into this. I'm sure it's none of my business. Now then, I think we'd best get along. It wouldn't be right for us to stay here and pry into family matters. I'm certain they'll work this all out on their own." He took a step then stopped. He reached up a hand and touched his bare head. This caused him to knit his brow. "Wherever did I leave my hat?" he asked himself. He strode into the barn with Emma at his heels. His hat sat atop a horizontal beam that ran along the rear wall. "That's right," he puffed at Emma, "I set it down to take hold of you when you were fumbling with the matches. It was very bad of you to nearly cause me to lose it. It's a very nice hat, you know."

Emma didn't bother to pin him to his contradictions. He seemed a singularly senseless person to her, and she had learned from some of the boys in preschool that it was pointless to attempt to reason with a senseless person.

The Gatekeeper took up his hat, but he waited until he had walked out of the barn to replace it atop his head.

Emma followed him. Outside, he turned his steps in the direction from which they had first come. Emma cast a concerned glance over her shoulder, but she could see no sign of the girl or the man who went yelling after her. Perhaps they were both in the house. Though she wished to save the girl from whatever punishment lay in store for her, she knew there was no way for her to do so. She couldn't speak to them. All she could do was haunt them with phantom touches. That wouldn't help anybody.

She walked up the gentle grassland slope beside the Gatekeeper. They spoke no more as they retraced their footprints in the snow. Emma had many questions, but she knew he would only respond to them with his silly talk that didn't come anywhere near answering her. She didn't like his silly talk, except that it made him less frightening than he might have been. It made these weird dreams less frightening too. His silly talk might be, she thought, the only thing keeping them from becoming real nightmares. If so, there was some good in it after all.

They walked until they reached the last of their footprints. They took another step and Emma woke up in her bed. It was morning.

Chapter 5

Emma put the spoon down inside the empty bowl. Marcia didn't usually make ice cream sundaes for dessert unless it was a special occasion, but it wasn't anybody's birthday today. Emma's mother made the best sundaes in the whole world, which was why it was such a treat for just an ordinary day.

Emma's parents had smiled at her all through dinner. Marcia talked to her so sweetly that she had to ask to make sure it wasn't her birthday after all. Rob assured her it wasn't, which left Emma wondering why everybody smiled and talked like honey to each other.

When everyone finished dessert, Marcia gave an extra smile and nod to Rob before turning to Emma. "Emma, we've got something we want to tell you."

Emma had been growing suspicious since before dessert. "Am I in trouble for something?"

Rob chuckled. "No. This is good news. It's very good news."

"Oh, good," Emma said.

"When you were in preschool, I went to the doctor's office," Marcia told her. "And guess what?"

Emma didn't know anything good that could be learned in a doctor's office. "What?"

Marcia took hold of her hand. "We're going to have a baby!"

Emma's eyes lit up. "I'm going to get a little sister?"

"Maybe. We don't know yet if it will be a boy or a girl. Maybe you'll have a brother."

Emma's shine faded a little. "A brother? Didn't you ask the doctor for a girl?"

"Honey, you don't get to choose between a boy or a girl. Besides, I think you'd really enjoy having a baby brother."

Emma weighed the idea. "Well, maybe. Just as long as he isn't a Mr. Bossypants, like some of the boys at school."

"With a big sister like you, I bet he'd be just about the sweetest boy there is."

"Well, that's true," Emma agreed.

"And I have something else to tell you," Rob said. "It's not as exciting as getting a new baby, but it has to do with our family."

"What?" Emma asked.

"We're going to visit your great-grandpa next weekend."

"I have a great-grandpa?"

"Yes, but he's very old, and he lives in a nursing home four hours away. He stays in bed most of the time, and he can't really talk so good anymore. We were afraid he might seem scary to you when you were younger, so that's why you never met him."

"Is he a hundred?" Emma asked.

"Almost," Rob answered. "And he's not doing too well lately. So, now that you're older, I thought this might be a good time to meet him, before—well—before it gets too hard for Mommy to take a long car trip."

Marcia turned in her chair, letting go of Emma's hand and taking hold of her by both arms. She turned Emma to face her squarely. "Honey, you don't have to stay there a long time if you don't want to. If you don't like it, we can go for a walk while Daddy visits, okay?"

Emma's expression changed to a pained one in an instant.

"Is something wrong, sweetie?" Marcia asked.

"You're squeezing my arms."

Marcia let go. "I'm sorry. I'm just a little nervous about this visit. I don't want it to frighten you. I didn't mean to hurt you, honey."

"You didn't hurt me. You just reminded me of my dream when you grabbed my arms like that."

"Did you have a bad dream last night? Was that what's-his-name man in it again? Did he hurt you?"

"The Gatekeeper. Yeah, he was there. He grabbed me by my arms, but it didn't really hurt. It was just a little scary."

"Do you want to talk about it?"

"It was pretty much like the other dreams. Only, he didn't ask about you guys this time."

A shiver ran down Marcia's back. "He asks about us?"

"Not this time. Before, he would sometimes ask me to bring you with me. But I don't want you to come."

"Why not?"

"It's not very nice there."

Marcia shot a look at Rob. "You think we should have her talk to somebody about these dreams?"

Rob asked. "Emma, do these dreams upset you very much?"

"A little bit, when I'm dreaming them. But not after I wake up. Except last night was scarier."

"What happened last night?"

"He made me do something I really didn't want to."

Rob leaned forward, showing Emma she had his full attention. "What did he make you do?"

"He made me start a fire. And there was a girl there too. And she got blamed for it, I think. I felt really bad for her because it wasn't her fault. The Gatekeeper was just being so mean to her."

"Tell us all about it."

Emma recounted her dream to them.

When she was done, Rob asked. "How do you feel about the dream now?"

"Well, I was a little bit sad when I first woke up, but then I remembered when I was little and had a bad dream, and you and Mommy told me dreams can't hurt anybody. I wish I didn't have them, but they don't really hurt me."

"Would you like to talk to somebody about them?"

"I am. I'm talking to you and Mommy."

"I mean somebody who knows all about dreams and stuff. There are people who are experts at talking to kids about things like this and making them feel better about it."

Emma shook her head. "I'd rather just talk to you and Mommy."

Rob winked at her. "I'm glad you like to talk to us."

Before anyone knew it, they were talking about the baby again.

Chapter 6

Emma opened her eyes in the dark. She was more annoyed than anything. Up to now, the Gatekeeper had given her a few nights of undisturbed rest between his visits. If he were going to make a habit of visiting every night, she could see herself getting angry with him. She didn't like him that much to begin with. If she'd ever heard the saying, she would have agreed that familiarity breeds contempt.

Hat in hand, he led her down the stairs. Something deep inside told her she had no choice but to follow him. It was her duty to go with him, as he'd said. This strange sense of duty she couldn't understand compelled her to go.

At the bottom of the stairs, he performed his invisible magic to open the door in the steps. He motioned for her to go ahead of him through the gate. She wished he would go first. That way, she could push him through and slam the door closed behind him. But she didn't know how to close the door, so his going first would do her no good anyway. She stepped through.

She came into a small room with a window in the facing wall. A curtain swung closed in the doorway behind her. The Gatekeeper did not follow. She turned around and separated the curtain with her hand to peer back. On the other side of the curtain was not her stairwell but a small kitchen with white appliances, more rounded at the corners than those in her house. Among the metal-legged table and chairs of the kitchen, the Gatekeeper was not to be found.

As she removed her hand from the curtain and faced the room in in front of her, she discovered she was holding a chipped, porcelain saucer in her other hand. On the saucer sat a stained porcelain cup filled with tea.

She seemed a great deal taller than she had always been, as if she were standing on a stool. She looked at her legs. To her surprise, they went all the way to the floor from beneath the flower pattern dress that extended halfway down her calf. She was taller. Her feet were bigger too. So were her hands, and so was everything else about her.

The room was lit by two floor lamps sprouting from metal bases, steadied by claw-like feet. There were two chairs and a sofa in the room, all upholstered in a different, faded pattern. Together with the mismatched end tables, the chairs gave the room an appearance of ancient neediness. All the apparently scavenged pieces of furniture were kept clean and dusted in a display of defiant pride. Through the window, Emma could see it was dark outside.

Beside the window hung a small, framed mirror. As soon as Emma saw this, she was drawn to it by an overpowering desire to look at her own face in it. It was hung too high for a child, but recent evidence persuaded her that this would not prevent her using it. She set her beverage down on one of the end tables and stepped in front of the mirror.

A face stared back at her. The face was hers, but at the same time, not hers. It was the face of a grown woman. The woman had dark hair like Emma, but with faint hints of gray here and there. Her eyes were Emma's eyes, only sadder and with the first sprouts of wrinkles spreading from their corners. The gray hair and wrinkles portended age, but the eyes themselves held the innocence of youth, making it difficult to gauge the woman's age. Somehow Emma knew it. The woman was near the age of Emma's mother, but she had lived a more difficult life.

The mouth, the nose, the chin, all shared a passing resemblance to the ones Emma was used to seeing in the mirror. The eyes were a perfect match. Without a doubt, they were her own eyes. Yet they were much older and careworn. The longer Emma examined the face, the more it seemed to belong to her. Or maybe it was that she belonged to the face.

Wearing this altered face did not startle her. With every passing moment, it became more natural that she should be wearing it. The consciousness that owned the face seeped into her and she became comfortable that everything here was in its proper place, including herself. This was her home.

She lived alone. She had no friends, few acquaintances. She felt more comfortable alone. No one asked her about where she came from, or why she left, or how she wound up here. She didn't have to explain anything to anyone. This made her solitude golden. She would work hard all day and sit alone every night. That, to her, was a good life–the best she could imagine, all things considered.

Emma sat in the chair beside the table where she had set her tea. She glanced around the room at the strange furniture, surprisingly familiar, trying to piece together in her mind how it was that she could be two people at once. She crossed her legs and took a drink of her tea. It wasn't sweet, like the kind of drink Emma would normally like, but she enjoyed it nonetheless. She liked it because the woman liked it, despite Emma's tastes.

At last, Emma gave up trying to reconcile her condition. The woman took over, and Emma became merely an observer, one who knew the thoughts of the observed subject. The woman took another sip of tea. She sighed as she replaced the cup on the saucer. There was little feeling in her sigh. It was as though she sighed because that was the thing she did at exactly this time every evening.

As if the sigh were a cue to action, the woman reached down under the end table and extracted a thick book. She set it in her lap and began flipping the pages. It was a scrap book, filled with yellowing newspaper clippings. Occasionally, the woman would stop on a page and examine a clipping for some minutes before moving on.

There were photographs as well. Most were of people dressed in old fashioned clothing. One was of a man in a suit beside a lady in a white dress. They looked so young and happy together. She calculated the year, as she did every time she saw this photograph. This was about five years before she came to them. In fifteen years, they would be old and broken by the strain she caused. They would never know the truth of her innocence. They would never fully trust her again. She wouldn't get the chance to revive their faith in her.

The woman felt a wave of emotion examining this photo. It was a confusing wave, filled with tremendous love and raw bitterness.

Emma could not recognize the people in the pictures, but she could feel the emotions they stirred within the woman. Most of the people pictured raised resentment in her, some of them crossing into absolute hatred.

The hatred reached its zenith when the woman turned the page to a newspaper photo of a solitary man. It was a head and shoulders shot, like Emma had seen in the book of presidents her teacher gave her on her birthday. The man had combed-back, smooth, grayish hair. His face was square and his jaw set. He stared directly into the camera with a smug look, like he was the smartest man in the world.

The woman's body shook. She mumbled at the picture. "If only you had minded your own business and left us alone. We could have fixed everything and been a family again. You ruined everything. If I broke them, you broke them more. You called yourself a doctor. Doctors are supposed to help people, not hurt them. Why couldn't you just leave us all alone?"

Emma felt the woman's urge to hit the man in the photo, but he was just paper now. Instead, she flipped the page and slammed his face down against the other pages of her past.

At last, they came to a photo Emma recognized. It was the little house and farm she had visited with the Gatekeeper. The woman's hatred melted away when they came to this image, replaced by a strong nostalgia for something loved and lost forever.

The woman stopped on an article that had no photographs. Emma sensed she always ended on this one. There was something in the settled way she came to it that would have hinted this much to any observer. It was the end of memories, a sort of living tomb for her. She began to read.

Emma had not learned to read yet, but the woman's mind translated the ideas to her. Though she had ignored the headlines of the other articles, the hurt this one caused spelled it out for Emma. *Caledonia Mills Fire Spook has Mental Capacity of a Small Child* the headline declared. The woman squeezed her eyes closed for several seconds after she read it.

When the woman opened her eyes again, she scanned the page, her mind quickly translating the words she read to Emma. There was a sense that she had read this page hundreds of times before. She didn't look at all the words, rather her eyes sought out particular words and phrases. She knew exactly where to find them. They were in the same hurtful places as always.

The first words transmitted to Emma comprised the name, Mary Ellen MacDonald. The woman cringed at reading the name, proof it indicated a person very near to her. Yet, everything about her way of living said that she had no close friends or relatives. It was her own name, the one she shared for this moment with Emma.

More words filtered through to Emma. The phrase *Fire Spook* made the woman grit her teeth so hard Emma could feel the pain.

It became clear after a while that the words on the paper were those of people giving their assessments of Mary Ellen; none were flattering to her intelligence. Words like *delusional*, *bereft*, and *nonsensical* occurred one after another. Through the eyes of this woman, Emma understood the meanings of them all perfectly well, and they made her unhappy.

The woman was even less happy. Tears ran down her cheeks. The woman moved the book on her lap to ensure that her tears did not smudge the ink. Though Emma's urge was to rip up the page entirely, she was not in charge. The woman guarded the page, and the pain it held, as if it were a precious relic.

At last, the woman's eyes neared the bottom of the article, where they settled upon one last damning quote. "Mary Ellen MacDonald appears to have mental abilities similar to those of a four-year-old."

The woman snapped the book closed and set it back in its place. She stood up and searched the area around her for something. Not finding it, she shrugged, and as if giving in to the assessment she'd just read, wiped her nose on the sleeve of her dress. Emma felt her mouth say, "That's fine. Four-year-olds don't need handkerchiefs."

This solitary act of defiance seemed to help. The woman stopped crying and moved on to the next step of her routine. She rose and walked to a beat-up Victrola in the corner. It had seen many brighter days and many happier owners. It still wound well, though. The woman bent over and wound the crank with gusto, no doubt as part of the regimen to release her nightly angst.

The lid was broken off, so there was nothing to lift in order to get to the turntable. A record was already in place, spinning at full speed. There were no other records to be seen, and the woman did nothing to indicate that there might be other choices. She lifted the stylus arm and moved it out over the spinning disk, setting the needle down at the outside edge of the record with the precision of nightly repetition.

From somewhere in the battered wood, below the turntable, a scratching noise emanated. It lasted only a second or two before being drowned out by music. If the sound of the music itself were not enough to tell Emma it was old, the method of producing it certainly gave her this clue.

The music began only as an instrumental, with no vocal element. It was music that Emma was unlikely to hear in her everyday life, with no lyrics yet to give her a hint of the nature of the song, yet she thought she recognized it by the melody. Somewhere in the back of her mind, this arrangement of notes had been stored. Even before the words, she knew this song.

The woman returned to the chair. She began to reach for her tea, but then stopped, shaking her head like the beverage had lost all its pleasantness to her. Instead of taking the cup, she sat down, drawing her knees up to her face and hugging her bare shins. She rocked a little, even though the chair was not a rocker.

Now the instrumental introduction was over. A man's voice sang along to the music. The woman mouthed the words along with him.

> *"Yesterday, upon the stair,*
> *I met a man who wasn't there.*
> *He wasn't there again today,*
> *I wish, I wish he'd go away..."*

Emma was sure she knew this song, only she wasn't sure how she had learned it. It hadn't come from her parents or her school, or anything else she could easily identify. She'd heard the Gatekeeper sing it once before, but now it seemed like the Gatekeeper had only been reminding her of a song she had already known. It felt like this knowledge came from somewhere deep within her, like she had been born with it. She seemed to know it just as well as this woman, who, she now had no doubt, listened to it every night.

There was a second verse, which the woman and the voice from the furniture sang together. Then, they went through both verses again before the instruments took charge once more and brought the music to an end. The music was replaced by static with a rhythmic skip in it as the needle hopped between the innermost groves of the disk. The sound was anything but pleasant, yet the woman did not show any inkling to attend to it. She sat with her knees against her cheeks, staring into the dark past. Emma felt grateful that she could not see the visions inspiring this woman's troubled memories.

The skip in the static slowed, as if the sadness in the sound had grown weary. The record ceased turning altogether. Still, the woman stared ahead of her, rocking back and forth. While there was music, or the book to look at, Emma didn't mind her connection to this woman. In the silence she felt trapped. There was nothing upon which to focus, save for pain, and the pain was closing in on her.

She wanted to scream, but she couldn't. The woman would not scream. She had forsaken screaming long ago. Now she would suffer in silence, rocking the pain until it fell asleep inside her for another night. Rocking it until it would let her get up from her chair once more.

Emma wanted to rise from that awful chair, but she had too little control over this body. At last, she felt herself growing in strength relative to this strange woman. She was able to stand up. She made her head turn and look behind the chair, not knowing what instinct led her to do so.

There, in the doorway to the kitchen, stood the Gatekeeper, with the cloth that hung there parted for him, seemingly of its own accord. He smiled a devilish smile at Emma and beckoned her with his finger.

Emma made the woman walk toward him. The Gatekeeper turned and went back into the kitchen. Emma followed him through the doorway, where she found herself alone, in her own body, in her own bed.

Chapter 7

"Do you really think this is a good idea?" Marcia asked.

Rob didn't look up from the road. "Whadaya mean?"

Marcia glanced over her shoulder to where Emma was watching a video in the back seat. She lowered her voice. "Taking her to see him?"

Rob gave her a quick look. "Why shouldn't we?"

"Well, it's just that he's so old and frail. Didn't they tell you he was usually only semi-conscious? I'm afraid he'll scare her more than anything else."

Rob reached over and patted her on the leg. "We talked about this with her already. It'll be fine. She's seen old people before. And he's not just any old man. He's her great-grandfather. One day she'll be happy she got to see who he was."

"But to see him like this? Will that be of any value to her?"

"Let's let her decide that."

"Yeah, if we knew he was still mentally aware. What if he does something that freaks her out? I mean, she's already having weird dreams."

"Marcia, one has nothing to do with the other. He's her great-grandfather, not some crazy dream figment. He's not going to do anything. You said it yourself: he's only semi-conscious. She'll spend a few minutes in the room with him, then we'll go and have a nice dinner with my cousins, and she'll always have the satisfaction of knowing she got to meet her great-grandpa. This will be important to her. She has no grandparents. This is her last chance to see one of her ancestors in real life."

Marcia checked to see that Emma was still paying attention to her video. "Well, at least let's look in first. Then we can decide if he's—it's—too scary for her."

"Okay, but we already know he's very old and he's probably going to be hooked up to an IV tube and stuff. It has to be something a lot scarier than that to nix the visit."

"All right," she sighed. "I just don't want to throw her into a situation she's not comfortable with."

"Neither do I," he said.

Two hours later, they checked in at the front desk of the nursing home. The lady pointed out how to navigate the hallways to the room they sought. They began to walk down the long corridor.

Having secretly listened to her parents' debate in the car, Emma worried about what kind of horrible place this could be. It was a great relief to find it wasn't very scary at all. There was plenty of light, and the hallway seemed well-kept. The people she saw in the hallway seemed normal enough. The only thing that was off-putting was the smell. It wasn't a disgusting smell, but it wasn't exactly a pleasant one either.

At last, they found the right door. Rob knocked with one knuckle. There was no reply. "Think we should just go in?" he asked Marcia.

"I guess. But be quiet. He may be sleeping."

"I hope it's a private room," Rob said as he pushed the door open.

It looked like a hospital room. A curtain was pulled around the center. Rob tiptoed in and peaked through the break in the curtain. To Emma it seemed like it took him a long time to decide. Finally, he waved his family into the room.

"It's him," he whispered as he led them beyond the curtain. "I can't tell if he's totally unconscious or just grabbing a little nap, so let's be quiet."

The first thing they noticed as they passed the curtain was how bright it was on the other side. The drapes had been pushed back from the windows, letting the full afternoon sun into the room. In spite of this, the man in the bed slept as soundly as if it were the dark of night.

His spotty complexion, wrinkled head, and thin gray hair told Emma he was very old. He was not pretty to look at, but he was not the monster she had constructed in her head after hearing her parents in the car. He didn't even look like a robot, which is what Emma imagined after her dad had said he would probably be hooked up to something. She'd thought he'd be plugged in like a machine.

He was just a sleeping man, who looked old or sick, or maybe both. Emma felt sad for him.

Rob took Emma's hand and led her to the side of the bed. "Emma, this is your Great-grandpa Shrudnick. He's my grandfather."

Emma surveyed the old man's face. She wasn't sure what to do, so she said, "Hello, Great-grandpa Shrudnick."

She didn't expect him to reply, but she didn't know what else to do, so she waited. After a minute, she turned to her father. "Will he wake up and talk to us later?"

"I don't know, sweetheart. In a while, I'll go see if I can find somebody to tell us how he's doing. Then we'll have a better idea if he can talk to us."

Marcia stepped up behind Emma, encouraged that her daughter was not afraid of the man in the bed. She touched Rob on the elbow. "Why don't you tell her a little bit about him."

Rob started in at once. "Well, Emma, your great-grandpa was a brave man. He fought in World War II. He was a paratrooper. That's a soldier who jumps out of a plane."

"He looks too old to be a soldier, or to jump out of planes."

Rob smiled. "That was a very long time ago. He was quite a bit younger then. In fact, he was younger than me and Mommy. He was practically a boy."

"Did he get shot in the war?"

"No. But he won some medals. I think I have some old pictures of him in his army uniform at home. Would you like to see them sometime?"

Emma nodded. At the same time, they heard a gentle tapping at the door. They looked at each other, not sure if they should be the ones to tell the person knocking to come in.

Before they could decide what to do, the door swung open and a woman in a nurse's uniform walked around the end of the curtain. She stopped short when she saw the three of them. "I'm sorry," she said. "I didn't know he had visitors."

"That's okay," Rob told her. "I was just telling my daughter about him."

"You're not his usual visitors," she said as a note to herself.

"No. Those would likely be my cousins," Rob said. "I'm one of his other grandsons."

"It's just, being here every day, I get used to the faces that come into the rooms," the nurse explained by way of apology for thinking out loud at them.

"We're from out of town," Rob said, bowing his head a bit. "We don't get to this part of the state very much."

The nurse smiled and nodded. It was the best she could do to relieve him of the feeling of being judged.

Rob turned to study the old man's face. "Do you know if he ever talks anymore?"

"No. He's usually just like this. It's been months since he's spoken to even the people he sees most." She grimaced to herself. "The nurses and the aides, I mean."

"That's too bad," Rob said. "I was hoping he could talk to my daughter a little."

As the nurse tended her patient, Emma's parents asked questions about his condition. Emma didn't understand most of this talk. She drifted away from the group and soon found herself on the other side of the room, looking out the window.

It was such a nice day, she felt like whistling, only she didn't know how to do that. A bluebird frolicked in a tree outside. It reminded her of a different bluebird she'd seen somewhere. She couldn't remember where. It was on a label of something, but she couldn't remember what. She tried to picture it in her head, but the details escaped her. All she could conjure was the outline of the bird against a black background. Then the bird label began to turn round and round until it all became a blur.

Without realizing it, she began to sing. The words were soft, but clear. They drew the attention of the three adults on the other side of the room.

"Yesterday, upon the stair,
I met a man who wasn't there.
He wasn't there again today,
I wish, I wish he'd go away..."

They were not the only ones who heard her. When Emma had finished her little verse, the lips of the man lying in the bed began to move. His eyes were still closed, and his body did not shift, but his mouth spoke. More than that, it sang.

"When I came home last night at three,
The man was waiting there for me
But when I looked around the hall,
I couldn't see him there at all!"

His adult listeners didn't have anything with which to give his words context except that he sang them to the very same melody that Emma had used. They stared at Great-grandpa Shrudnick with their mouths open. Then they raised their heads in unison and stared at Emma, their mouths no more closed than before.

Emma stared back at them. She was no less shocked than they were to hear the old man continue her song. She approached the bed, waiting to hear if he would sing more. She'd always assumed that the song was a part of her dreams. She hadn't ever imagined hearing somebody in the real world sing it.

Great-grandpa Shrudnick settled back into his sleep. The nurse broke the silence. "Well, I've never heard him do that before," she said. "We never thought to sing to him."

Rob had recovered from the shock and was eager to try again. "Emma, sing that song one more time."

Emma looked sheepish. "I only know the first part by heart."

"Okay. Just sing the first part, then."

Emma repeated her verse. This time there was no response from the bed. Rob had her sing it twice more, without success.

At last, Rob shook his head in sadness. "That's too bad. I thought he might be coming out of it for a minute. It would have been nice to talk to him."

They stayed with him for a while longer. It was only in the car on the way to meet his cousins that Rob asked Emma about the song itself. She gave him the same answer about it that she had given her mother. She hated to admit that she had heard it in her dreams, because now it was a real song in the real world. She didn't like the idea of there being a connection between her weird dreams and the real world.

She could honestly say she didn't know how she and the great-grandpa she'd never met came to know the same song that nobody else in her life had ever heard of.

There was one thing she did know. She recalled where she had seen that bird spinning around on a label. She remembered reading the word *Bluebird* arched across the top of the record label, even though in real life she couldn't read.

Chapter 8

Emma followed the Gatekeeper down the stairs. It had been almost a week since he'd come. She was grateful for the respite.

At the foot of the stairs, the Gatekeeper did his subtle magic, opening the doorway to the other place in the steps. They went through it, and Emma found herself on the snowy slope above the farm. She walked toward the farm buildings as a matter of course, the Gatekeeper beside her in the gloomy daylight.

At first, they went in silence, as they usually did. Before they had gone far, he spoke to her. "Mary Ellen, my dear, have you told your parents about your visits to this wonderful place?"

Emma preferred silence with this companion, but something told her it was best to answer when he made inquiries. "A little," she said. No one said the answers had to be long ones.

"Did you mention how much you enjoy coming here?" he asked.

"No." She didn't enjoy coming here at all, but that was more than she wanted to say to him.

He sighed. "That's a pity. You should tell them what fun we have here. Maybe they'd like to come with us one of these times."

Emma could think of only one reason to bring her parents here: to chase this annoying man away from her. Since he was a dream man and her parents were real people, she doubted their ability to do so.

"I don't think my mother is supposed to be out in the snow like this. She's having a baby." The moment she said it, something in her gut told her she shouldn't have.

"I know," he said. It almost sounded like a growl, and he showed a lot of teeth when he said it. "But I don't think this snow would hurt her. You don't even feel it on your feet, do you?"

43

Emma didn't answer the question. Instead, she said, "I don't think they would like it here."

The Gatekeeper issued a small chuckle but there was no joy in it. "Silly child," he said. "Of course they would. This is a fine place. Ha, ha. Of course they'd like it here."

She did not respond.

He touched her on the arm firmly enough to stop her. "I really think you should invite them." His tone relayed that it went beyond a pleasant suggestion.

"If you want them to come so bad, why don't you just show up in their dreams and bring them?"

He raised his eyebrows. "Dreams?"

Emma nodded. "Yes. Just like you do with me. Just like we are now."

He gave her a little grin of belated comprehension. "For one thing, people must come here willingly, and as unfortunate a fact as it is, it's harder to get adults to do the things you want them to. They can be very stubborn when it comes to people and places that lie beyond their limited understanding of the universe." He shook his head with a wistful smile.

If he were going to talk such nonsense, Emma had no advice for him. He'd have to figure out how dreams worked for himself.

He folded his arms across his chest. "No, my dear, it is you who would have the most success bringing them here. And as for dreams, well, we'll see about that in the fullness of time. But for now, think as you wish. If it speeds us toward our ends, so much the better. Let this be the world of your dreams."

Emma didn't understand exactly what he was trying to say, so she kept quiet and let him finish. None of his gibber-jabber would matter in the least after she woke up anyway.

Seeing what little effect his words had, he nudged her forward with his hand and resumed his march alongside. The rest of the way they went in silence. Emma was happy for that.

The barn door was open, but the girl was not inside. The pile of hay they had set alight was considerably smaller than it had been. Emma wondered what prank they would play today. Would they untie the cows, or make braids in their tails? She hoped it would be something of this nature, because she didn't enjoy burning things. That was too dangerous.

Out of routine, she veered toward the barn, but the Gatekeeper caught her arm. He shook his head at her and then nodded toward the house. At first, Emma resisted. The people she'd seen before were more likely to be found in the house, and she didn't want to see them. She didn't like being around people who couldn't see her. It felt weird. And she especially didn't want to tease the poor girl as they had done the last time. That was just mean.

The Gatekeeper's pull was too strong, and when Emma reflected that nobody really got hurt in dreams, she relented. They went in the door at the back of the house. The room they came into was a kitchen. It was not like any kitchen Emma knew. She deduced that the cast iron bulk against the wall was a stove, the glow from inside indicating a fire within. There were some cupboards, a wash basin, and a bit of plain countertop supporting Emma's conclusion about the room.

In the middle of the room, stood a small, round table with a kerosene lamp burning on top of it. Seated at this table was the girl they had previously met in the barn. She had a book propped open and was meticulously copying down a lesson from it on a piece of slate. The volume of marks on the slate indicated she had been at it for some time. Her head bobbed as she struggled to shake off the sleep that stalked her labors.

As had been the case in the barn, the girl could not see them. Nor had she noticed the door open and close as she was sitting with her back toward it. Oblivious to any other presence within the room, the girl worked at her slate, even as her head sunk lower toward the table.

"You're not going to touch her again and make her all scared, are you?" Emma asked.

"Oh no," he assured her, making his denial with a very serious face. "Not right off, anyway," he added with devilish curl of his lip.

Emma tried to make her voice stern. "I don't like it when you do that."

He ignored her, going on with his own thoughts. "Poor thing. She's so terribly sleepy. Let's let her get some rest." He hummed a lullaby and the girl stretched out her arm across the table and rested her cheek on the inside of her elbow. She closed her eyes and let the piece of slate chalk fall from her fingers.

"Sleeping like an angel," he cooed. "Such an evil little angel. The source of so much mischief. Sleep, Mary Ellen, sleep. Your friends will help you be naughty. What else are friends for?"

He took hold of the kerosene lamp.

Removing the glass tube surrounding the wick allowed him to raise the wick itself from the basin of fluid beneath. Holding the burning wick in one hand, he shook the basin toward the wall. The lurching liquid made violent splashes against the wallpaper.

Emma stepped backward. The liquid from the lamp smelled bad, and she certainly did not want any of it spilled on her clothes. Added to this concern, she knew what the Gatekeeper was doing was wrong. She couldn't tell exactly what he was up to, but she was old enough to know you didn't just go around making messes on the walls in other people's houses.

The Gatekeeper didn't spill all the liquid, but he was satisfied with what he had done. He replaced the wick, bringing the ebbing flame back to life with a fresh slurp of kerosene. "Careful there, child," he told Emma as he set the lamp down on the table. "You nearly backed clear into the stove there. But, no matter, we need something from the stove anyhow."

He strode past Emma and opened the door of the stove. Emma saw red hot coals glow beneath the burning wood inside. He reached in. Emma slapped a hand over her mouth to suppress a shriek.

To her surprise, he did not scream or even grimace in pain. Rather, he rooted around with his arm halfway disappeared into the cast iron hulk. His face wore no expression of pain, but one of somebody searching for something with only his sense of touch. At last, a light of satisfaction flickered in his eyes. He extracted his arm from the stove, eager to examine the object he felt in his hand.

When his hand emerged, it held a burning stick of wood. The stick was only as wide as a bottle cap and just a bit longer than the ruler Emma used in school. It burned at the end opposite his hand. Whether the near end had been aflame when he grabbed it, Emma could not tell, but a thing like that would not surprise her anymore in this strange place.

The Gatekeeper held out the stick toward Emma, signaling her to take it from him. She shrunk back from it and shook her head.

His frame slumped with exaggerated disappointment. "Oh, don't be afraid. It won't burn you. Look, this end wasn't even in the fire." He showed her that his end was unburnt.

"No. I don't want it," Emma said. "You'll make me do something bad with it."

"Nonsense!" The words came out like spit. "I won't make you do anything of the sort, so long as you be good and take it like I ask."

"I don't want to."

"Take it, child. Before I have to resort to harsh words." He thrust it at her.

Emma truly did not want the torch, but the way he waved it at her made her feel that she might be safer with it in her hand than in his. She reached out her timid fingers.

He passed her the torch, nodding his approval. It was a relief to have him do something other than scold her, but she understood that this respite must be fleeting. The man grinned and nodded toward the wall where he had spilled the kerosene.

Emma frowned. "I told you you'd make me do something bad."

"I'm not making you do a thing," he said with uncharacteristic calm. "I haven't laid a finger on you. You'll do it because you know you must. You'll do it because you want to. You see, everything depends upon you doing this. It's your duty, you understand."

Emma hesitated. He was wrong. She didn't want to do it. At the same time, a new feeling was welling inside her. Some invisible force pulled her toward the wall. For an instant, it seemed like she had done this before, and she would do it again. She would do the thing the man wanted done simply because it was her role to do it.

"Hurry now!" he bellowed. "Before the flame dies out."

Emma stepped to the wall. It was wrong, but there seemed no other choice. She touched the remaining flame against the drenched paper. The burst of fire, eating at the wall in all directions, startled Emma; she jumped backward.

Emma bumped hard into the table, knocking the girl's book to the floor with a loud thud. From an adjoining room, someone called out. "Mary Ellen, you all right in there?"

Mary Ellen didn't answer. She slept soundly, head down on the table, despite the jolt Emma had administered.

Emma heard footsteps approaching. She knew the Gatekeeper heard them too, by the weird look he got on his face. It was an impish look that said with thinly veiled delight, "Uh oh. Somebody's about to get in trouble!"

The flames climbed the wall, throwing a ruddy glow onto the sleeping girl's face. The Gatekeeper looked down into that face and shook his head at her ruefully. "Tsk, tsk," he began, "such a very naughty girl. Well, it sounds like it's nearly time for Mary Ellen to face the music." He slapped her outstretched arm hard enough for the blow to make a sharp noise. It was more than sufficient to wake the sleeper.

The girl shook the sleep out of her head. She appeared heartily confused when she noticed the fire eating away at the wallpaper. In an instant, her eyes grew wide and she let out a short shriek. She kicked the chair out from under her and stood facing the flaming wall, her frame shaking with panic. At one instant she looked ready to spring forward and fight the flames; in the next instant it seemed certain she would do nothing but stand there and shake until the entire house burned down around her.

A figure appeared in the doorway to the next room. It was the old man they had seen going into the barn. He recognized the danger at once and yanked the cloth from the table. Pushing the girl behind him, he beat the flames with the tablecloth, all the while demanding from the girl, "What have you done? What have you done?"

The girl, in her terror, did not reply. She stood in the doorway watching her father attack the flames.

Emma watched her. She got a good look at the girl's eyes. They were familiar. They looked very much like the eyes she had seen in the mirror at the apartment of the lady with the scrapbook. For the first time, Emma felt a bond with this girl, similar to the one she had felt with the lady. The bond went beyond sympathy for the injustice being done her. It was a bond of kinship.

At last, the man made headway against the fire. He whacked at it with vigor until the last flame was vanquished. He surveyed the blackened wall for a moment, then turned and tossed the cloth down on the table. Inevitably, he settled his gaze upon his daughter.

Tears filled Mary Ellen's eyes, and it was easy to understand that her greatest urge was to run away. Yet, there was a light of simple wisdom behind her tears, and this wisdom deemed it best for her to stay.

Her father pointed toward the door through which Emma and the Gatekeeper had entered. "Go fetch me a switch!"

Mary Ellen, overcome with sobs, shook her head and took a step backward into the next room. Her tears did nothing to soften her father's resolve. He took a purposeful step forward, staring his condemnation at her. She understood the look and ceased her retreat. She could not retreat far enough to avoid what was coming. She scurried across the kitchen floor and slipped through the outside door, letting it bang closed louder than good judgment would have dictated.

At the noise, Mary Ellen's mother appeared in the doorway to the next room. She was younger than her husband, but still older than Emma's parents. She wore a plain, white dress that covered her from neck to ankle. "What's all the commotion in here, Alex?"

Alex stood to the side so his wife could see the blackened wall behind him. "Look here, Janet. That girl is up to her evil ways again. She nearly burned down the whole house, and with both of us inside. Is this our reward for giving her a good home and loving parents?"

The woman put a hand over her mouth. She bowed her head and squeezed her eyes shut as her hand slipped down to press against her chest. "Dear Lord, Alex, what are we to do?"

"I'll tell you what I'll do, Janet. I'll whip her to within an inch of her life. And I'll do it over and over again until I chase The Devil out of her. That's what I'll do."

The outside door opened just enough for Mary Ellen to squeeze through it. She didn't raise her eyes from the switch in her own hand, even after she had closed the door behind her.

"Give me that!" Alex snatched the switch from her. "I'm resolved to teach you the wickedness of your ways, girl, and one way or the other, I will teach you."

Mary Ellen's head drooped as her father tested the flexibility of the switch.

"That's two fires inside of a week. First you try to burn down the barn, with all my livestock in it, then you try to burn up your own parents in their own home. I don't even know what to say about it. Best I let this here switch do my talking."

Mary Ellen dared not look at her father. Instead, she appealed to her mother. "No! I didn't do it! I swear, I didn't start them fires. I didn't do none of it. I was just sleeping here at the table when something woke me up. The wall was already on fire when I woke!"

Janet stood still. She wanted to believe her daughter, but there was something in the way Mary Ellen stood rigid and upright that would not allow even a welcomed gullibility.

The girl threw her arms around her mother's neck. "Oh, Ma! You got to believe me!"

Alex stepped forward and pulled the girl off her mother. Janet flinched one time but made no motion of resistance thereafter.

The Gatekeeper put a hand on Emma's shoulder. "This has all been interesting, but it looks like they've got things under control now. I think it's best we leave them to their family business."

Emma scowled at the Gatekeeper. She hated what they'd done. But it could not be undone now, and she did not want to see what would happen next. As Alex took his family into the next room, Emma and the Gatekeeper went out the back door.

Chapter 9

Rob hadn't even closed the front door behind him when Marcia grabbed him by the arm. "Come with me," was all she said.

Rob let himself be pulled along. "Where are we going?"

"Upstairs."

"Where's Emma?"

"At a play date."

At the top of the stairs, it became clear Marcia was leading him to their bedroom. "I like where this is headed," he said with a smile. "We should send Emma on more afternoon playdates."

"Don't get too excited. It's not what you think." She led him into the bedroom, past the bed, and to the desk at the far wall. Their computer was on the desk, with a page loaded on the web browser. A video was cued up, but it was not playing yet.

"What's this?" Rob asked.

"This is *The Little Man Who Wasn't There*."

Rob made a confused look. "What?"

"Remember when we were visiting your grandfather, and Emma started singing that song, and then your grandfather went on with it out of the blue?"

"Yeah. Of course I remember it. That was kind of freaky."

"It was really freaky," she corrected. "And that's not the first time Emma's sung that song. I picked up on some of the words, and it's not the kind of song a five-year-old would normally sing. I don't think they would teach it in preschool. It's spooky—about a ghost or something. I asked Emma where she learned it. She told me she learned it in these dreams she's been having. Well, I don't know how you learn something you don't already know in your dreams, so I thought it must be something she made up in her dream. But

52

then your grandfather convinced me it was a real song, so I searched it. Listen."

She clicked on the play icon for the video. The video was nothing more than a static shot of an old record sitting on a record player. On the label in big letters was the word *Bluebird.* This was all Rob could read before the record began spinning. The stylus arm came down on the edge of the disk and music played. It was old-fashioned music, played by an orchestra of different types of horns.

Rob waited to hear whatever it was that Marcia so badly needed him to hear. So far, the music meant nothing to him. He read the title below the video out loud: "Glenn Miller Orchestra. *The Little Man Who Wasn't There.*" The music continued without vocals. "Glenn Miller," Rob mused, "I've heard of him. I think he was big during World War II."

Marcia shushed him. "Listen."

Over the music, somebody started whistling. After a few bars of this, two men began having a conversation. One of them addressed the other as Tex. In a scripted intro to the song, Tex explained that he had just seen a chilling sight. Then Tex began to sing the song.

Marcia knew every word by now. Rob only faintly recognized the gist of the lyrics and the melody.

They listened and watched the video of the record spinning until the needle hit the inside part of the disk and the music ended. "What do you make of that?" Marcia asked.

"Well, it explains how my grandfather knew the song, anyway. He probably listened to all kinds of records like that when he was a kid."

"But it doesn't explain how Emma knows it."

"She must have picked it up somewhere."

"Yes. But where? She told me she heard it when she went with the Gatekeeper."

"The guy in her dream?"

"The one who takes her to that strange place through a hole in the stairs."

"It doesn't seem likely she learned it in a dream though."

"No, it doesn't seem likely. It seems creepy. I don't like her dreaming about some weird guy all the time, and I don't like her singing old songs about ghosts that nobody younger than eighty has ever heard of."

"Okay, yeah, it's a little creepy on the surface of it, but I'm sure there's a reasonable explanation. I mean, old songs just don't come to kids in their sleep like that. She probably just doesn't remember where she really heard it."

Marcia put up her hand to interrupt. "Wait. There's more. When I searched for the lyrics, I discovered something else. This song was originally a poem." She looked down at the note pad she kept by the computer. "It was written by a guy named William Hughes Mearns in 1899. It's called 'Antigonish,' after a town in Nova Scotia where they apparently had a problem with ghosts on stairs."

"But Emma doesn't know about all that, does she?"

"I don't think so. But it bothers me that she says this Gatekeeper takes her through a door in our stairs. And he takes her to a place that's cold and gray. Isn't Nova Scotia cold and gray?"

Rob shrugged. "I don't know. I've never been there."

"It just all fits together too well. I don't like it."

Rob put his arm around her. "Hon, don't you think maybe you're making too much of this? Isn't it possible Emma heard that old record somewhere and then formed part of her dream around it? Maybe it's not as strange a coincidence as you think. A lot goes on in that little head of hers. She's a pretty creative kid."

Marcia sighed. "Maybe. I don't know. I just wish she'd stop with these recurring dreams and singing spooky old songs out of the blue."

Rob leaned his head against hers. "I bet it will all be forgotten in a couple of months."

"I sure hope so."

They heard the front door open. "Hello? Marcia?" a woman's voice called out from below.

"We're upstairs, Beth!" Marcia shouted to the familiar voice.

"I'm dropping Emma off," Beth yelled up to them. "Just wanted to make sure somebody was home. I can't stay. Gotta pick up Jack from soccer. Talk to you tomorrow."

"Okay. Thanks so much. See you tomorrow."

The downstairs door closed. Emma ran into her parents' room. "Hi Mommy! Hi Daddy!"

Both parents gave their daughter a hug. Emma saw the computer screen beyond them. "You listen to the Bluebird record too?" she asked.

Marcia stiffened. "What do you know about Bluebird records?"

"I listened to it in my dream."

"Who played the record in your dream?"

"A lady did." Emma squinted as she considered. "Or maybe it was really—it's hard to explain. There was this really sad lady, but it's kind of like I was inside her. She drank tea and looked at old pictures for a while, and they made her so sad."

"Was she on the farm with the girl who got blamed for the fire?"

"No. She was someplace else, but it might have been the same girl, only different. Like she was more grown up. And her parents weren't with her anymore."

"What else did she do besides look at pictures?"

"Nothing really. Except just sat there and stared at things and felt sad. Then she played the Bluebird record, and that was about the end of the dream."

"What was the Bluebird record she played?"

"It was the song about the little man who wasn't there."

Chapter 10

Emma woke in a strange bed. She first realized it was not her own bed because the window was not where it was supposed to be in her room. Instead of a window draped with cartoon ponies across from the bed, there was a blank, off-white wall. There was no window in any of the walls. All of them where the same miserable color.

The ceiling was the same color. From it protruded a single light bulb, encased in a metal cage. The bars of the cage threw lines of faint shadow on the walls. Emma disliked those shadows. She didn't know why, when she first noticed them, but she knew they bothered her. She watched the shadows as she sat up in the bed and took stock of her surroundings. As she grew into wakefulness, the shadows became more familiar, and she understood why she hated them. Unlike shadows created by sunlight, they never moved. They stayed the same, day or night. The light was always on. She couldn't tell when it was day and when it was night. She hated that.

It puzzled her that she knew the shadows wouldn't move, until she swung her legs over the side of the bed. Then it made sense. Her legs were too long for her. Her arms were too long as well. Her hands were too big. This was not her body.

It was odd that the Gatekeeper didn't bring her here. She'd never gone to a place in these dreams without him leading her there. That was all right though. She was tired of his face anyway. If she had to go to weird places in her dreams, it was just as well she didn't have to endure his unpleasantness too.

As Emma came fully awake, the room around her grew familiar. She'd never been to such a wretched place before, and yet she knew all the parts of it. There weren't many parts to know. There were the bare walls, the lightbulb, the door with the little covered window, and her bed. Besides these things, there was only her.

The bed was little more than a frame, bolted to the wall. A bare mattress, a wool blanket, and a flat pillow made up the bedding. It wasn't comfortable, but she got used to it. It seemed like she got used to it, anyway. Emma wasn't sure how she could have done so, since she usually slept in a nicer bed, but still, she possessed a knowingness that she had gotten used to it.

She realized that she hadn't awakened naturally. She had been disturbed by the sound of footsteps approaching and stopping at her door in the hallway outside. She stared expectantly at the little covered window in the door.

The cover moved back, opened from the outside. The eyes and nose bridge of a male face appeared in the opening. The eyes settled upon Emma. "Good day, Mary Ellen! I'm glad you're awake. It's Wednesday. Time for our weekly chat!"

Though the voice surrounded its words with eagerness, even a child could hear the disingenuousness. Emma said nothing, because Mary Ellen said nothing. Emma could see, but only Mary Ellen could speak.

The window slid closed. Sounds of jangling keys came through the door. A key was inserted into the lock and the door opened inward.

The man who came in had a head too small for his body, or a body too large for his head. He bore scruffy whiskers all over his face, too much jowl for a man his age, and he emitted an unpleasant odor. His long, white coat hung from his shoulders in an uneven, slovenly manner.

He brought a chair and a clipboard with him. Sliding the chair in front of the bed, he sat down.

Mary Ellen wore white as well. Hers was a lightweight gown with very short sleeves. It didn't go down past her knees and it felt uncomfortably drafty. The draft was uncomfortable, not because it was cold in the room, but rather because it accentuated just how embarrassingly flimsy the garment was.

Mary Ellen attempted awkwardly to pull the gown in all directions at once as the visitor stared and smiled at her. He seemed amused by her futile attempts toward modesty.

Mary Ellen hated the way he looked at her. His half-smile every time she looked uncomfortable made a shiver run up her spine. It magnified her discomfort and made her reluctant to interact with him. She knew she was supposed to speak to him, so she did, when it felt necessary, but she did not like it.

She did not like him. He stared at her too much and asked her the same questions every time he came. He didn't believe her answers. That was clear from the faces he made and the way he questioned them as if they were ridiculous hoaxes. Then he asked the same questions again next time. He didn't fool her. She had him figured out. He thought he could wear her down and make her give up the lies and finally tell the truth.

It wouldn't work that way, because Mary Ellen was telling the truth all along. If he ever did wear her down, he would end up making her give up the truth and start telling lies. Sometimes she thought that was what she should do. Maybe if she told him the fake stories he wanted to hear, he'd go away and stay away for good. Maybe that's what he really wanted. Maybe if she gave him the right lies to write down on his paper, that would be the end of it.

It was tempting to give him his precious lies and see what would happen, but Mary Ellen's parents had taught her a lie was a sin. She'd rather suffer the badgering of this horrible man than anger God, or worse, disrespect her parents.

Emma sensed all Mary Ellen's thoughts. They strengthened her bond with her host. Mary Ellen was good. Emma had always known that was true, but now she was more confident about it than ever. This was a scary place, but Emma was glad Mary Ellen was doing the right thing, despite their shared fears.

Mary Ellen ceased pulling at her gown. There was no way to make it cover her sufficiently, and fussing with it only made the man stare at her more intently as his wicked half-smile grew. She folded her hands in her lap and bowed her head.

The man crossed his legs and rested the clipboard on his thigh. "If you're done arranging yourself, may we begin?"

Mary Ellen shrugged.

"Did I tell you how pretty you look today?" the man asked.

Mary Ellen suppressed a cringe. He said something about how pretty she was every time. She hated it. For one thing, she knew she wasn't pretty. She was very plain. She'd always been very plain, and that wasn't such a bad thing. She shuddered to think how he would look at her if she were actually pretty. On top of that, there was no kindness in his voice when he said those words. It didn't sound like a compliment. It sounded like a trick. He was trying to make her like him more, but the kind of person who tells you you're pretty, when they don't believe it, was not anyone she wanted to like.

Her hands slid apart and formed themselves into fists on her lap. "Stop saying I'm pretty! I'm not pretty! I'm perfectly plain!"

He reached out and softly ran a thumb from her ear to her chin. "You're pretty to me, Mary Ellen."

She pulled her head away from his thumb.

He sighed and brought his hand back. "Ah well. I'll save my tenderness for when it's appreciated."

Mary Ellen tensed her arms and flexed her fists. She didn't know what he meant by that, and she didn't want to know.

"Well then, if you insist on getting right down to business, we'll get down to business." He cleared his throat. "Tell me, Mary Ellen, why did you start the fires?"

Mary Ellen's head snapped upright, shifting her gaze from her hands to his face. Her eyes narrowed in anger. "I told you, I didn't start no fires! I don't know why you ask me the same questions every time when I already told you the answers to all of them!"

He gave her another half-smile. "You give me answers, all right, but you never answer my questions."

"What's that mean? Why must you forever talk riddles at me? I give you answers, and that means I answer your questions. I always answer your questions, but you don't like my answers, so you keep asking—"

"I'm just trying to get at the truth, Mary Ellen."

"You got at it already. I told you, I didn't start them fires."

"All right. You didn't start the fires. Who did, then?"

"I don't know."

He tapped his pen on the clipboard. "Tell me, Mary Ellen, who else could have started those fires? Was there somebody else in the barn with you, in the kitchen, any other place a fire started?"

"I don't know."

"Well, did you see anyone else?"

"No. I don't know."

"Yes or no?"

"No. I didn't see nobody."

"Then who could have done it? A ghost?"

"Maybe. Who knows?"

He shook his head at her. "Come now, Mary Ellen. You expect me to believe a ghost started the fires? And would you also like me to believe he chose to do so when only you were present?"

Mary Ellen set her jaw. "You can believe what you want to. All I know is I never started no fires."

The man shifted in his chair, as if shaking off their unproductive beginning. "All right, Mary Ellen, let's leave the fires alone for a while. We'll go back to simpler things. Before the fires began, who kept letting the livestock loose from the barn?"

"I don't know."

"Was it you?"

"No."

"Letting a few cows out is no serious trouble. If you happened to let them out for a lark, no one would be angry with you. It was just a little joke, that's all."

Mary Ellen's shoulders slumped. She could tell him she'd let the cows loose. It was just a little lie. It might be worth a little lie to have him leave her alone about one thing, anyway.

Emma fought the wilt in Mary Ellen's spine. Mary Ellen had done none of it, and it was wrong for her to say she had. If she gave in on this, who knew but that she wouldn't be admitting to all of it in another minute, just to make the man go away.

Emma tugged at Mary Ellen's resolve from the inside, willing her to use her tongue to refute all blame. Still, Mary Ellen sat silent.

The man wagged his pen at her. "Wasn't it just a little joke?"

Mary Ellen slowly lifted her head. She sat up tall. "That's not the kind of joke that's funny to me."

"What was it then?"

"You should find whoever did it and ask them."

The man sighed and shifted. "Come now, Mary Ellen. You can admit you let the livestock out. It's all right. It was innocent enough. No one will say a cross word to you about it."

"They got no reason to say a cross word. I never did none of that."

The man wrote a note on the clipboard. His face seemed to darken. "All right, Mary Ellen. We've made no headway on the fires. We haven't even made headway on the livestock. Therefore, let's talk a little bit about your parents, shall we?"

Mary Ellen recoiled. "No! I don't like to!"

"We won't have to, if you'll tell me about the fires."

She straightened herself. "I already told you a thousand times. I don't know nothing about them fires."

The man shrugged. "Then we'll just have to converse about your parents a little. What became of your parents, Mary Ellen?"

"I don't know."

The corners of the man's mouth turned up. "You don't know? Maybe you just don't want to remember."

"I can't. I can't remember."

"Let me help you. Think back."

"I don't want to! I don't want to remember!"

The man made a subtle nod, but neither Mary Ellen nor Emma could tell why. "If you want to get well, you must remember, Mary Ellen. You'll never get out of here if you just cover over your memories—the things you were responsible for. Think back with me. Your parents blamed you for the fires, didn't they?"

Mary Ellen sat stone-faced, neither nodding nor shaking her head.

"They blamed you for the fires and they punished you," the man went on. "Your father spanked you and whipped you with a stick, didn't he?"

Mary Ellen did not twitch.

"He whipped you harder each time, didn't he? It hurt you more every time. The pain didn't go away so easily after a while, did it, Mary Ellen?"

He waited for a response, but he got nothing more than a cold stare from her.

"They hurt you more and more, and you resented them for it. They shouldn't hurt you for something you didn't do, should they? But they did. They blamed you for the fires and they beat you for it. You grew to distrust them. They were supposed to protect you, but they beat you instead. In time, you despised them. And then what happened? What happened, Mary Ellen?"

"I told you I don't know!" she screamed. "Stop asking me about them!"

"You're lying, Mary Ellen. You do remember. You're pushing it down inside of you." From underneath the clipboard he produced an oval looking glass. He held it up by the handle protruding from the bottom. The man held it out like a spotlight pointed at Mary Ellen's face. "Look at yourself, Mary Ellen. Look into your own eyes and see if you can find the truth there. Study yourself and tell me if you see the face of truth or lies in the mirror."

For the first time, Emma saw the face she wore in this rendition of her strange dream. It was the face of the girl who the Gatekeeper had tormented in the barn. It was the face of the older woman who had looked through old scrapbooks in her lonely apartment. Yet it was exactly neither of them.

The face in the mirror was older than the girl in the barn. The eyes held the same fear of the world around her, but the face surrounding them was more mature. The lips were fuller and the cheeks less round and childish. The nose was better defined, and the jaw set more firmly.

The face was younger than the woman in her little apartment, and less careworn. The eyes shared the anger of that woman, but there were no traces of gray in the dark hair. There were not so many lines chiseled into the skin on the forehead and around the eyes.

Behind all these comparisons to the younger and older versions of this woman, Emma saw the glow of her own eyes. She did not want to be part of this pitiful woman, young or old. It hurt too much to wear these faces. Emma now understood that for as long as she looked at the world through these eyes, the hurt would never end.

Emma wanted to cry. She was not alone in this. A tear ran down the cheek she saw in the mirror. It brought relief to no one.

Emma forgot about the man behind the mirror until he spoke again. "Look deep into those eyes, Mary Ellen, and tell me they don't remember. Can you lie to your own face?"

"Leave me alone!" Mary Ellen cried. "Why can't you just leave me alone?"

The man let the mirror down. "You'll curl up into a little ball and die in here if I leave you alone. You have to face the past if you ever hope to overcome it."

"It doesn't matter anymore!" Mary Ellen insisted. "It's all over and done with, and it can't be undone."

"That's true, Mary Ellen. The past can't be undone. But what about the future? You can't face the future honestly if you don't come to terms with your past."

"I have no future!" Mary Ellen spit out. "Everybody already made up their minds I'm bad. Ain't nothing I can do about it now. I'm that bad girl who did all them bad things. That's what they all say about me. Even the newspapers say it. I seen them. Nobody's ever gonna think anything different of me now, no matter what I do. So there ain't no use talking about it anyhow."

The man slid from his seat onto the bed beside the girl. He laid a hand on her back. "Now, now, dear girl, you mustn't think that way. Not everyone believes you're bad. I don't believe it. I think you're a good girl. You want to be a good girl, don't you?"

Mary Ellen sat frozen by the feel of his touch on her back. His words echoed and garbled themselves as if they came from the far end of a narrow pipe. The feel of his hand on her back dominated her senses. It didn't belong there. Maybe he would take it away if she stayed perfectly still.

Emma didn't understand. This man who had been scolding Mary Ellen now acted much nicer, but through Mary Ellen, it gave Emma a strange feeling of foreboding. She couldn't say why it didn't feel better to be comforted than reprimanded, but it didn't.

The man's hand moved. He rubbed a small circle on Mary Ellen's back. "I like you, Mary Ellen," he whispered. "I don't think you're a bad girl. Wouldn't you like to show me how good you can be?"

Mary Ellen sat still and held her mouth shut. She wished he'd go back to yelling at her. His whispers were far more frightening.

The man used his free hand to take hold of Mary Ellen's chin. He turned her face toward him. "I know you want to be good for me. Deep down inside"—he breathed at her—"you long to be good for a man like me."

He peered into her eyes, holding her frightened gaze as he moved his lips toward hers.

She shrunk from him, but he held her firmly. His lips moved closer as he shifted his weight to compensate for her retreat. She felt his breath on her face.

Retreating only made her more vulnerable as he rose above her in his pursuit. The man's actions, first so puzzling to Emma, now terrified her. Her fear merged with Mary Ellen's fear and spurred a spontaneous convulsion in the latter.

With both hands Mary Ellen gave her attacker a violent shove. He fell backward, slipping off the bed onto the floor. She watched in desperate terror as he toppled.

His face was red when he looked up at her. His eyes narrowed and he clenched his teeth. "You'll be here a long time, you stupid bitch! If you don't understand when someone is trying to help you, you just might die here."

He climbed to his feet, collected his things, and dragged his chair toward the door.

Mary Ellen's eyes followed every movement.

"I won't be so nice next time," he told her.

He was leaving. That was all that mattered. Tomorrow might be a far worse day, but he would leave her alone for today. Today was all that counted. Tomorrow would be a new battle, with a doubtful result, but tomorrow wasn't nearly as important as today.

After he went out Mary Ellen listened until she heard the key turn in the lock. Then she lay back on the bed, closed her eyes, and let the peaceful nothingness of her empty world wash over her.

Emma woke up frightened and confused.

Chapter 11

Emma had been exceptionally quiet during the ride home from preschool. When they entered the house, Marcia invited Emma to snuggle up next to her on the couch. Emma loved to snuggle with her mom. It seemed just the thing she needed.

Marcia stroked her daughter's hair. "Miss Perkins told me you've been kind of mopey in school lately."

"Yeah," Emma answered in a tone devoid of inflection.

"And I've noticed you haven't exactly been all smiles around here too much either. Is something bothering you?"

"I guess."

"Would you like to talk about it?"

"I don't know."

"I promise to be a good listener."

"Okay. We can talk about it if you want."

"Good. I'm all ears. Tell me all about your troubles."

Emma turned her eyes toward Marcia's face. "You might think it's dumb."

"I don't think anything that worries you is dumb."

Relief shone through Emma's eyes. "That's good."

"Now tell me about it."

"Well, I know it's only a dream, but I really don't like having to go with the Gatekeeper anymore."

"I don't blame you. He doesn't sound like the kind of guy I would want in my dreams."

"Yeah, I really don't like him very much."

"Tell me all about it, sweetheart."

Emma frowned. "He makes me do bad things. I don't want to do them, but he makes me."

66

"You mean like when he made you start a fire?"

"Yes. And he made me start another one in the house. But that's not the worst thing."

"What's the worst thing?"

"At the place where he takes me, there's this girl. I told you about her. She's a lot bigger than me. She's probably in sixth grade or something. The Gatekeeper likes to get her blamed for starting the fires. And it's not even her fault. I started them."

"But he made you."

"Yes. He tells me to do it, and I don't want to, but I know I have to. He says it's my duty, but I think he means he'll do something bad if I don't."

Marcia frowned. "Something bad to who?"

"I'm not sure. I don't know if he'll do something worse than ever to the girl or do something bad to me. Everything just always gets worse. The first time, he made me put braids in the cows' tails and let them loose. Then he made me start a fire in her family's barn. Last time, he made me start a fire in her house. Her parents thought she did it and she got in big trouble. So, I don't know how bad the next thing will be."

"Why do you think he makes you do these things to her?"

"I don't know. I think he's just a rotten person. I don't like him."

"He sounds very mean."

"He is. And he calls me Mary Ellen, even though I keep telling him my name is Emma. I know he hears me, but he just doesn't care."

"Mary Ellen?"

"Yeah. Mary Ellen."

"I wonder where he got that from? Do you know any girls named Mary Ellen from school?"

"No. I don't know anybody named Mary Ellen. Except—"

"Except who?"

67

"Except the girl in the other place. I think her name is Mary Ellen too. The Gatekeeper tried to tell me that she was me, but that's too silly."

"It's very silly." They were quiet for a moment. Then Marcia said, "Tell me about the place he takes you to."

Emma told her about the snowy field, the barn, and the house. She went on the describe the girl called Mary Ellen and the man and woman who were Mary Ellen's parents. She retold the stories of all the pranks she and the Gatekeeper had pulled on poor Mary Ellen, all the time stressing that she wished they would stop doing such horrible things to a girl who had never done anything to them. She explained that none of the people of the place could see her or the Gatekeeper, though she felt certain the animals knew they were there. She concluded with the wish that the Gatekeeper would stop taking her there, because it didn't seem like the sun ever shone or anybody was ever really happy in that cold place.

"Does the Gatekeeper ever call the place by a name?" Marcia asked.

Emma thought back. "No. We don't talk about it at all. It's just the place we go. I have two places. I have here, with you and Daddy and my friends, and then that's just the other place. But sometimes I go to even more different places."

"You do? Like where?"

"I don't know where they are for sure. Remember the lady I told you about, who played the Bluebird record? One time it was like that lady's house, but it wasn't a big house like ours. It was just a little house for one person. Last time I went to this place like a jail or something. It was really scary. I didn't like it at all."

"Was Mary Ellen in those places too?

"Yeah, she was there. I mean, I'm pretty sure it was her, but it was weird. It was like I was inside of her looking out through her eyes."

"Did the Gatekeeper do bad things to her?"

"No. Not those times. He was hardly even there."

"Well, that must have been better."

Emma shook her head. "No. Not really. It was worse. I saw everything she saw, and it just made me sad the whole entire time."

"What made you feel so sad?"

"I can't tell you, exactly. I guess it just felt like nobody in the whole world loved me, and nobody would ever love me. It was so lonely. I hated it."

"I'm sorry, sweetheart. But you know, in real life, you have lots of people who love you to the moon and back."

"I know. That's why I feel so bad for Mary Ellen. She doesn't know what that's like."

Marcia squeezed her daughter. "If that's the case, I feel bad for her too."

Emma sighed. "I don't want to go back. It just makes me sad. I don't like going to any of those places."

"I wouldn't like it either. It doesn't sound very pleasant."

"That's what I told him."

"Told who?"

"The Gatekeeper. He wants you and Daddy to come there too, but I said you wouldn't like it."

"He wants me and Daddy? Why?"

"I don't know. He just does. Maybe he wants to call you Mary Ellen too. He's kind of a weirdo."

"Emma. . ." Marcia began to chastise her daughter for calling names like that, but she thought better of it. In this case, she'd let it go.

"What, Mommy?"

Marcia altered her next statement. "Would you like to talk to somebody about these dreams? I mean, somebody who talks to kids about this kind of stuff all the time and can make you feel better about it."

"I did already, Mommy."

69

Marcia's body stiffened. "You did? Who?"

"You, Mommy. You talk to me all the time about stuff, and you always make me feel better."

"Do you feel better about your dreams?"

"Lots."

Marcia hugged her close. "I'm glad. Listen, if you can find a way to come and get me, in your dream, before the Gatekeeper takes you to the other place, I'll go with you. I'll straighten up that Gatekeeper so he doesn't bother little girls. Okay?"

Emma smiled up at her. "I'd like that, Mommy."

Emma's smile should have brought Marcia relief. Instead, it brought her the realization that she had gone a step too far. Of course, she couldn't guarantee what she would do in someone else's dream. As much as she wished her presence could reassure her daughter, it was a mistake to make promises. She worried she had just made matters worse.

Marica stewed all day about having overstepped. When Rob came home, she took him aside. "I think we should have Emma see a psychologist."

"Her dreams are getting worse?"

"It seems that way. I think they're really starting to frighten her."

"Did you ask her about going?"

"She thinks she's fine just talking to us about it, but it's time we made some decisions for her."

"She may not like that. She's a pretty strong-willed kid."

"The key word is kid. She doesn't understand how harmful this could be to her. We do. It's time for the adults to step in and take some of this off her shoulders."

"All right, then let's step in."

"I'm going to look for a psychologist tomorrow. I wish I'd started on this sooner. I just hope she doesn't have a dream that completely freaks her out tonight."

70

Chapter 12

A soft touch woke Marcia. She could just make out the silhouette of someone standing beside her bed in the darkness. By the shape of the silhouette, if not from the gentleness of the touch, she knew it was Emma.

"Emma, what's the matter? Did you have a bad dream?" she whispered, to avoid waking Rob.

"This *is* my dream," Emma replied. "Remember? You said you wanted to come with me next time."

"I remember."

"Well. It's time."

Marcia rolled out of bed and put on slippers and a robe. She was too groggy to contemplate the intricacies of being in her daughter's dream—if that's really where she was. All she knew was she had made a promise to Emma and she would do her best to keep it.

She followed Emma out of the room. In the hallway they met a short, slim man. As part of this bizarre, shared dream, it seemed perfectly natural that he should be waiting there. In the dark, Marcia couldn't make out any of his features. All she could judge of him was the shape of his silhouette and the darkness of his dress. He held a hat in his hand. No one spoke. The man nodded slightly, showing satisfaction that Marcia had come with her daughter. Marcia needed no introduction. This silhouette was the Gatekeeper.

The Gatekeeper stood back to allow the others to go downstairs ahead of him. At the bottom, he turned his back to them and practiced his invisible magic on the stairs. The steps rose, allowing the hollow light beneath to seep through. The tainted light cast shadows at the man's face, illuminating nothing of his countenance. If this silhouette had human eyes, Marcia could not see them. The

71

shadow of a man made a motion with his hand toward the light. Emma took her mother's hand and together they went through.

Marcia's hand was empty when she emerged from the portal. It felt natural that it should be. She found herself entering an office of some sort. The striped paper on the walls jabbed at her senses. The room smelled of wood polish.

A man, dressed in a tweed suit, sat at a roll-top desk. He faced away from the doorway in which Marcia stood. He was busy writing something, and consequently did not see that someone had come across the threshold. He turned his head when he dipped his pen into an inkwell, showing a ruddy complexion on his cheeks and wire spectacles over his eyes.

Out of the corner of his eye, he spied Marcia and immediately put down his pen. "Oh, Mrs. MacDonald. I didn't see you there. My humblest apologies. Won't you please come in?"

Marcia stood still. She didn't know to whom he was speaking. She expected this Mrs. MacDonald to brush past her into the room, but no one did.

The man at the desk raised his eyebrows. "Mrs. MacDonald? Won't you come in?"

Marcia turned her head the slightest bit and peered over her shoulder. There was no one in the doorway but her. She stepped into the office. As she moved, she realized she was wearing a dress of light material rather than her robe or her pajamas. Leather shoes had replaced her slippers.

The man motioned toward a wooden chair opposite him. "Won't you please take a seat?"

Marcia nodded. Without the slightest prompting from her mind, her mouth said, "Yes. Thank you, doctor." As she stepped around him, she discovered they were not alone. Hidden from the doorway was another chair, occupied by Emma.

Marcia slid her hand behind her dress to keep it from bunching as she sat down. The chair creaked beneath her weight.

72

"I'm glad you came, Mrs. MacDonald."

Marcia guessed him to be her equal in age. He was well-groomed and his face tended toward handsome. There was a kindness in his eyes and gentleness to his voice.

Marcia was now convinced that he spoke to her when he addressed Mrs. MacDonald.

"There's somebody I wanted you to meet. This is"—he turned his head toward Emma—"Mary Ellen. She's staying at the home for orphans. I thought you two might like to get to know each other."

This was not Mary Ellen. It was Emma. A woman should know her own child anywhere. Though Marcia knew this, she was Mrs. MacDonald in this dream, and Mrs. MacDonald did not act like she knew it. Mrs. MacDonald acted as though she had never seen the child in her lifetime. She nodded toward the girl. "Very pleased to meet you, Mary Ellen."

"Pleased to meet you, Ma'am," the girl replied.

"She's a very well-behaved child," the doctor said.

"And so pretty." Mrs. MacDonald replied, smiling at the girl.

The girl lowered her eyes to hide her pleasure at the compliment.

"They have nothing but good things to say about her at the home. When I first met her, I thought to myself, who would take pleasure from meeting such a worthy child? And I thought of you straight off, Mrs. MacDonald."

"That's very kind of you, doctor."

The doctor waved it off. "Not at all. It's nothing but the truth." He reached into the vest pocket of his suit and pulled out a coin. He handed the coin toward the girl, saying, "Mary Ellen, here's a penny. Why don't you step next door and buy yourself some candy?"

The girl's eyes lit up. She slid from the chair and took the money. "Thank you, sir."

The man patted her head. She went out.

When she'd gone, he turned to face Mrs. MacDonald squarely. "Isn't she a lovely child?"

"Indeed she is."

"I thought you would think so. I was hoping you would like to spend some time with her. Maybe she could spend a day with you and Mr. MacDonald at your farm."

She gave a hint of a nod but said nothing.

The doctor sighed. "Mrs. MacDonald, it amounts to this. After you lost the last baby, I warned you against any further attempts to have children. In the state you were in, I wasn't sure if you took my words to heart. I need to make sure you understand your chances of carrying a child to full term are very small, and the next time you try, it could very well kill you."

She closed her eyes for an instant. When she reopened them, she said, "Yes. I remember."

"That's good. I know how badly you and your husband would like a child, but as your doctor, I needed to know that you would not risk your life for a dream beyond your grasp."

She stared at his face. Her mind was blank.

"But there is another option," he went on. "That's why I invited Mary Ellen to visit today. She, and many more like her, need caring parents. To put it plainly, Mrs. MacDonald, I'd like you to consider adopting a child."

"Oh"—her voice trickled out with little breath behind it—"I see."

"I know it's not the way you would prefer to have children, but I think you and Mr. MacDonald would find it rewarding. You have a lot of love to give to a child, and there are children like Mary Ellen who need exactly that."

She began to fidget. "Yes. Yes, I suppose that's so."

He gave her a pleading look. "I could arrange for Mary Ellen to spend some time with you whenever you wish. Or maybe one of the boys, if you'd prefer. I chose Mary Ellen because she's just such a delightful child, and she's younger—I believe she's five—I thought you would like a younger child."

74

"Well, I hadn't really thought—yes, I suppose a younger child would be best," she stammered. "But even such a small child seems—I'm not sure I would know what all to do with a five-year-old."

The doctor grinned at her. "Don't worry, Mrs. MacDonald. I'm sure you'll figure it out in no time. No doubt, Mary Ellen will help you with that."

The door opened and Mary Ellen came into the room. She was sucking on a piece of candy. The doctor put out his hand for her. She came near him and took it. "I have good news, Mary Ellen. Mrs. MacDonald has asked to spend more time with you." He guided her toward Mrs. MacDonald.

Mary Ellen released the doctor's hand and took a timid hold on Mrs. MacDonald's. "Thank you, Ma'am," she said.

Marcia could not speak as she gazed into the face that belonged to Emma, but a different Emma. She could not think of what to say to this girl who was her daughter, but not her daughter right now. What could she say when the part of her that controlled her actions was not even herself? She merely stared into that sweet little face and awaited whatever was next.

The doctor rose from his chair. He stepped toward them, breaking the spell that kept Marcia's gaze trained on Emma. He recaptured their attentions as he swept past them, but when they looked up to follow him out, they saw the back of a petite man wearing a black suit, with a hat in his hand.

Without turning back to show them his face, the man beckoned them through the doorway. Hand in hand, they followed. Together they stepped out of a dream.

Chapter 13

Marcia slid her hands over her belly. Wakefulness unclouded her mind, allowing her to understand the needlessness of her movement. It was just a dream. This woman with a history of losing her unborn children was a figment. It was not her. She was safe, home in bed.

But it was a disturbing dream. To dream she had become part of another's dream left her mind boggled. The details of the dream only added to her uneasiness. The details she remembered so clearly; she would not soon forget this one, and that was the most troubling thing about it. It was destined to be one of those handful of dreams that stick with a person for life.

She shook Rob awake. "It's time to get ready for work."

Rob rolled over and groaned his regular morning groan. "Where do these nights go?"

Marcia did not answer. She stared at him, envious of his peaceful night.

Rob blinked the sleep out of his eyes and pulled himself up onto one elbow. He squinted at her. "You all right, babe? You look kind of frazzled."

"I just had a strange dream. That's all."

"What about?" A light of revelation came to his eyes. "Shoot! Hold that thought. I've got to get in early today; we're having a staff meeting. Sorry. You can tell me about it this afternoon if you like, if you haven't forgotten it by then."

"I think I'll remember it."

Rob rushed into the shower and Marcia went downstairs to get the house going before Emma woke. Twenty minutes later, Rob was out the door and Emma sat at the kitchen table eating toast. Marcia joined her with a cup of coffee.

"I was thinking yesterday"—Marcia slid Emma's cup of juice away from the edge of the table—"that you only have a few more weeks of preschool. After that, it won't be long until you start kindergarten. You're getting to be such a big girl. Are you excited about going to kindergarten?"

"Yeah. I guess." She took a tiny bite of toast and chewed it a long time, as if it were much bigger.

"You'll meet lots of new friends."

"Yeah." Though she had swallowed her toast, Emma continued her mechanical chewing.

"Don't feel like talking this morning?"

She stopped chewing and looked at her mother's face. "Mommy, was I adopted?"

Marcia, at the point of taking a sip of hot coffee, gulped instead. The drink burned her mouth. She grabbed a napkin and spit into it. "Adopted? No, Honey, you weren't adopted. You came out of my belly just like the new baby will."

Emma smiled for the first time all morning. "Good. I'm glad I wasn't adopted."

"What made you ask such. . ." Marcia cut herself off. She knew what, and she knew Emma knew she knew what. The two of them looked at each other with pouty faces. This was complicated, and neither one understood quite what to make of it.

Emma broke the silence. "Thanks for coming with me."

Marcia nodded. "Sure. I told you I would, didn't I?"

"Yeah. I felt better having you with me, but I wish you didn't have to come."

Marcia smiled at her daughter. "I'll do whatever it takes to make you feel better."

There were a lot of things they might have discussed about the shared experience, but Marcia needed to think it through first. She had no answers for Emma about how such a phenomenon could happen. She had no answers for herself. They could compare notes later; first she had to figure out how to make sense of the overall occurrence.

When Marcia thought of anything else all day, it was how much she admired Emma's ability to put these strange dreams aside and be a normal person during the day. That she could not do likewise became obvious by the time Rob came home from work.

She pounced upon him the moment he opened the front door. "Oh my God, I've got so much to tell you! I don't even know where to begin."

"Tell me about what?" he asked as she dragged him into the living room and pushed him onto the couch.

"About Emma, and these dreams she's been having." She sat facing him and took hold of both his hands. "It's been driving me crazy all day."

"Okay? Where is Emma, by the way?"

"Another play date. I wanted to talk to you alone." Marcia found her starting point and dove in without delay. "Remember I showed you the poem I found online about the little man who wasn't there?"

"Sure."

"And remember how it was about that town in Nova Scotia?"

"Yeah, I guess."

"Do you remember the name of the town?"

Rob shook his head. "Not a clue."

"It's Antigonish."

"Okay."

"So, I was talking to Emma about her dreams the other day, and she told me this Gatekeeper guy keeps calling her Mary Ellen. He refuses to call her Emma; it's always Mary Ellen. And remember she said he made her do bad stuff when he takes her to that other place?"

"I remember she said he made her start a fire."

78

"That's right. There's a barn and a house there. He made her let the cows loose, and then he made her start fires in the barn and in the house."

"In the house too? I just remember her mentioning the one in the barn."

"The one in the house was afterwards." Marcia's eyes became misty. "I did a bunch more online searches today."

Rob put a hand on her knee. "You gonna be okay?"

Marcia gave him an uncertain nod. "Eventually, I put in the combination of Antigonish, Mary Ellen, and fires." She took a deep breath and picked up the note pad from the coffee table. "This is what I found. In 1922, a girl named Mary Ellen MacDonald"—her voice cracked on the last name—"became known as the *Fire Spook of Caledonia Mills*. She was blamed for starting fires in her parents' barn and house. Before that, she pulled more innocent pranks, like letting the cows out. But it was the fires that made her an international news story. She denied it all, to her dying day as far as I can tell, but there was no other logical explanation. Some people claimed she was possessed. She had to live with the stigma of being the *Fire Spook* for the rest of her life. Just reading about her gave me an incredible feeling of misery."

Rob scratched his neck. "Okay, it's a bit of a coincidence between the name and the fires, but this was in this Whatever Mills Place, not the town with the man who wasn't there."

"Rob, wait. I'm not done. Caledonia Mills is in Antigonish County, Nova Scotia. It is the *same place!*"

Rob made a move as if he were shaking off cobwebs. "There's got to be a rational explanation. How did Emma find out about all this? I mean, dreams are pieced together out of the leftovers of our conscious thoughts, right? She must have seen a TV program or something about this whole Nova Scotia thing and then had bad dreams about it."

"When would she have seen a TV show about it without our knowledge?"

"I don't know. But she must have heard about it somewhere. You don't dream about things you don't know about."

"Are you sure about that?"

"Well, I never have. Have you?"

Marcia wrung her hands. "If you'd asked me that yesterday, I would have said no."

He stretched his neck toward her. "But?"

She looked at the ceiling and pursed her lips before finding the words. "I went with them."

"With who?"

"Emma. And the Gatekeeper."

"What? What are you talking about?"

"I had the same dream as Emma last night. We were in it together. We both went with the Gatekeeper."

"No. You're not serious."

Her stare said she was.

"Are you going to tell me he made you start fires too?"

"We didn't go to the farm. We went someplace else—to a doctor's office. Emma was this girl, Mary Ellen. And I was, well, I think I was her mother."

"You're not sure?"

"Well, pretty sure. Remember what I said Mary Ellen's last name was?"

His eyes juggled words. "McDougall, or something like that."

"MacDonald. Her name was Mary Ellen MacDonald. The doctor kept calling me Mrs. MacDonald. Keep in mind I didn't discover her last name on the web until today. Yet, that's the name I was called in my dream last night."

"Maybe Emma told you the last name when she was telling you about Mary Ellen. Maybe you just forgot, and your subconscious saved it for your dreams."

80

"I'm pretty sure she didn't tell me that. But, okay, let's assume for the sake of argument she did. In my dream, I wasn't Mary Ellen's mother just yet. She was an orphan"—Marcia's eyes welled with tears—"and I kept having miscarriages."

She put her hands over her belly.

"The doctor told me I couldn't have children and he wanted me to adopt Mary Ellen."

Rob tilted his head. "I'm sorry. That must have been a disturbing dream. But what does it prove?"

Marcia wiped her eyes. "There's one more thing I discovered in my research today. Mary Ellen, known in her time as *The Fire Spook of Caledonia Mills*, was adopted by Janet and Alex MacDonald."

Rob whistled at the news. "Wow! That's downright freaky."

"And there's one more thing."

He shook off a heavier layer of cobwebs. "I'm not sure I'm ready for one more thing, but go ahead."

"This morning, when Emma and I were eating breakfast, she asked me if she was adopted. That's how I knew we were in the same dream."

"Did you ask her about it?"

"No. I didn't have to. We both knew we were in the same dream. We just knew. In fact, she thanked me for coming with her."

"Is she freaked out by it?"

"Not like I am. Maybe she's been having these same dreams long enough that she feels like whatever happens in them is perfectly normal. Anything can happen, as long as it's part of a dream. I don't think she knows two people don't usually have the same dream at the same time. She has no idea how creepy that is."

"That's good, right? I don't want her to be terrified." He rubbed Marcia's knee. "What about you? Are you okay?"

Marcia's head bobbled on her neck. She released a long breath. "I don't know. I suppose there has to be an explanation for all of this, but I'm still freaked out. I spent the afternoon on the phone with my mother, talking about it, and she wants me to have a priest come here. I don't think I'm quite ready for that yet, but if we go through any more of this kind of stuff, I may get there quick."

"Did you find a psychologist for Emma? Maybe you could go with her."

Marcia's eyes bulged at him. "Are you kidding? I can't take this to a psychologist now! How would we even begin to explain what's happening without looking like complete loons? Look, if I go in there acting like I really believe I participated in my daughter's dream, they'll lock me in a rubber room, and God knows what they'll do with Emma."

"You think it would be that bad?"

"Don't you get it? Everything's changed now. This is not just a little girl struggling with subconscious issues. This is—I don't know—some sort of supernatural phenomenon. We're miles past a psychologist now. We're racing down the road to my mother's priest."

He squeezed her knee. "There is an explanation, we just haven't figured it out yet." He blinked purposefully, as if inspired. "You said Emma thanked you? Did she ask you to go?"

"She's been asking us to go from the very first, she just didn't know she was. Remember the first time she talked about the Gatekeeper? She started the whole thing by asking when we were going to the other place. She hasn't pressed it because she's not completely sure about taking us there. She told me the Gatekeeper wants her to take us there, and I think that makes her nervous. She doesn't like it there very much, so she'd be more comfortable with her parents. On the other hand, she doesn't trust the Gatekeeper, and she's afraid he wants to hurt us. Anyway, when we talked about it, I told her to come get me when the Gatekeeper wanted to take her there, and she did. I don't know how it happened, but I was in her dream and she was in mine. And I'm pretty sure she felt better that I was there."

"If that's how it works," Rob said, "I'll tell you the same thing you told her. When this Gatekeeper comes to take you someplace, come and get me. I think we'll put an end to his bullying once and for all."

Marcia gave him a wan smile. "The problem is we're not really sure how any of this works just yet."

Chapter 14

When Marcia came downstairs Saturday morning, Rob was in the kitchen arranging sliced strawberries atop a stack of waffles. "I thought you might want something more than coffee and a muffin this morning," he told her when she came in.

"Wow, strawberry waffles! What's the occasion?"

"Oh, nothing. I just knew you've been feeling stressed lately, and I thought this might be a nice pick-me-up."

She kissed him on the cheek. "How nice. Thank you."

"And I broke the sink."

"You did what?"

He stared at the kitchen sink. "You know how the faucet's been dripping? Well, I thought it shouldn't be too hard to fix it. To make a long story short, I was wrong."

"What did you do to my sink?"

"I cleaned up most of the mess, and the water's turned off underneath, so don't try to use it."

Marcia couldn't suppress a frown.

"But the good news," Rob continued, "is that I found a plumber who'll come out today. He'll be here sometime within the next four to six hours."

Marcia rolled her eyes at his good news.

"And if that's not enough good news"—he lifted the plate he'd made for her—"there's also strawberry waffles."

Marcia rolled her eyes again, but playfully this time. She took the plate and went around the corner to the dining table. He followed with a plate he'd made for himself.

"Well, at least you don't look like you've had any disturbing dreams," he said after they were seated.

"No. Either the Gatekeeper didn't show up or they didn't bother to pick me up on the way out."

"Let's hope he found someone better to visit at night."

"That's worth hoping, but even with Emma he's taken plenty of nights off only to reappear at his convenience." She looked around the room the way people do when they know the object of their search is not there. "Where is Emma anyway?"

"I gave her some waffles already. Just for today, I let her eat in the TV room. She probably needs a little treat too. And I didn't know if you were going to have any more dream revelations you wanted to share with me alone."

The doorbell rang.

Rob got up. "If that's the plumber, that was quick. I just called fifteen minutes ago."

"Maybe he smelled the waffles."

Without the overalls and the big toolbox, the man at the door would not have looked the part of a plumber. Rob couldn't put his finger on exactly what it was that looked out of place, but it felt like this guy should be sitting at a desk, banging away at a keyboard instead of under a sink banging on pipes.

The plumber stood with a dignified, almost military, straightness. His hair was short and neatly trimmed and he was clean shaven to perfection. His fingers were long and well-kept, carrying the toolbox like it was a prop rather than his stock and trade. Altogether, he was the tidiest plumber Rob had ever seen.

Despite his look not fitting the stereotype, according to the patch on his spotless overalls that read *Capital Plumbing*, he was the plumber. "I'm here about the water basin pipes," he said, almost as a question.

The man's appearance and the words *water basin* left Rob addled for an instant while he translated them to mean *sink*.

"I'm the plumber," the man said, in a tone meant to provoke some response from the homeowner.

Rob shook off his confusion. "Of course. Come in. You're here about the sink."

"Indeed, sir."

"I'm happy you could come so quickly," Rob said as he led the plumber into the house.

"Yes sir. Our intent is to please."

"Well, so far, so good." Rob led him past the dining table, where the man gave a quick bow in the direction of Marcia, and around the corner to the kitchen sink. "Here it is. The water's off underneath. I'm afraid I messed up some of those pipes, but I guess you'll figure that out as soon as you get down there."

Rob half expected a lecture on leaving these things to the professionals, but he got none of that. All the plumber said was "Very good, sir. I'll start in at once."

"Is there anything I can do to help you?"

"Not at all. If you'd be good enough to go about your usual business, I'll see to this."

Rob went around the corner and rejoined Marcia at the table. She was enjoying a silent giggle.

"What?" he whispered.

"That's your plumber?" she whispered back. "He acts more like a butler than a plumber. All he's missing is a British accent."

Rob shrugged. "I guess he's a new breed of plumber. I kind of like him. Besides, he got here in no time. That's definitely a mark in his favor."

They took bites of their waffles between exchanging secret smiles about the characteristics of their plumber.

At length, something occurred to Rob. He leaned in and spoke in a low tone. "I was going to ask you something, before Jeeves"—he tossed his head toward the corner wall— "interrupted us."

Marcia covered her mouth to keep her last sip of coffee in as she giggled.

"I was thinking about what you told me about this dream you and Emma were in. When you were in the dream, did you know it was Emma, or did you think it was this Mary Ellen girl?"

Marcia's smile faded. "It's like a part of me knew it was Emma, but that part was in the background. A part of me was still me, too, but the part that was playing the role of Mrs. MacDonald was dominant. The me part couldn't really do anything except observe. Mrs. MacDonald did all the talking and made the decisions."

"Was there anything in the dream itself that indicated you were in this town in Nova Scotia?"

"No. There wasn't any big sign that said 'Caledonia Mills' or 'Antigonish' or anything like that, but it all fits in with everything I discovered online. Are you thinking it's just a huge coincidence or something?"

"I don't know what to think. That's why I'm trying to get all the information I can, so I can figure out what my theory is." In order to forestall the consequences of being judged a faithless skeptic, he jumped into another question. "What about Emma? Do you think she recognized you? Or was she too much of this Mary Ellen MacDonald girl?"

"I'm sure she recognized me, but whether she could do anything about it is another issue. She was probably in the background just like I was."

"Did she look normal? Or did she have some kind of crazy look in her eye, like she was this—what did you call it—fire spook?"

"She looked like she always does. Like a perfectly normal five-year . . ." Marcia trailed off and stared past Rob's shoulder.

Rob spun around to see the plumber standing at the corner. The man gave a half bow to them. "Forgive the intrusion, but your pipes are repaired."

Rob stood. "Already? That was quick."

The plumber turned to lead the way to the sink. "As it turns out, the damage was slight. Nothing that a few soft rings wouldn't fix."

Rob turned on the faucet and examined the pipes below the counter. "Looks perfect. That's nice work"—he looked at the name embroidered into the plumber's logo patch—"Eli."

"Thank you, sir, but it was hardly anything at all."

The plumber collected his toolbox, and they walked around the corner together. "How much do I owe you?" Rob asked.

"I'm sure it won't be much. We'll bill you."

Rob and Maria exchanged secret smirks at their good fortune. "Can we offer you a cup of coffee or anything before you go?" Marcia asked.

"No thank you, ma'am. But if I may be so bold, I couldn't help but overhear some of your recent conversation. It sounded quite like you were speaking of the Fire Spook of Caledonia Mills."

Marcia's jaw dropped. "You know about that?"

"Oh yes. I certainly do. You see, I have roots in Nova Scotia. The Fire Spook is an important part of the folklore where I come from."

"Really?" Marcia asked. "You know about the MacDonalds?"

The plumber shook his head in sadness. "Poor, unfortunate folks, the MacDonalds. Mind you, I don't know the details of the family. As you must know, these happenings took place many years ago. But it's said of them that they were good people, salt of the earth. The kind who don't deserve such as they got."

"And what about Mary Ellen? Do you know anything about her?"

"Not a lot. They say she was a regular girl, normal as a child could be, until those queer occurrences began."

"The fires?"

"Some other things too, but mostly the fires."

Marcia stared him in the eyes. "Did Mary Ellen start the fires?"

The plumber tilted his head and lifted his shoulders. "Well, there are people who will still debate that to this day."

"What do you think?"

The plumber made a show of leaning back from the question. "Oh, ma'am, I'm afraid I'm not the one to judge. There's many that

88

think one way, and many that think the other, and I suppose they've all got their reasons."

"It just makes no sense that a little girl would want to burn down her own house."

"That's exactly what I've heard some say. On the other hand, she was the only living soul found near about the fires. As I recall, they called in a sort of investigator. His name was Dr. Prince. He was a psychologist or some such. Well, the long and the short of it was that he concluded Mary Ellen was starting all these fires in some kind of somnambulistic state."

"Somnambulistic?" Rob asked.

"She was sleep walking," Marcia interpreted.

"Exactly," the plumber said. "This Dr. Prince blamed it all on the girl. Mind you, he said she wasn't in her right mind at the time, but he blamed her nonetheless. Well, in those days, when somebody with the word *doctor* in front of his name made a finding, lots of people thought it had to be the truth of the matter, and that was too much for poor Mary Ellen to climb out from under. It's said the poor girl never had another happy day the rest of her life."

"I came across Dr. Prince's name when I was reading about Mary Ellen." Marcia said. "You sound skeptical of him,"

The plumber scratched his cheek. "Well, since you put it that way, I guess I am, and always have been. I guess the MacDonald's biggest mistake was to trust the man. I wouldn't have done it, I'll tell you. Not with my daughter's life. I've heard Dr. Prince had some odd ways about him, and I'm inclined to believe it. He shouldn't have been trusted." The plumber looked Marcia in the eye. "I wouldn't trust him."

A shiver ran up Marcia's spine and she shook off the plumber's gaze. When she turned back to him, he was making sure his toolbox was clasped tight.

"Well, I guess I've wasted enough of your time, babbling on about ghost stories. There's plenty more work for me today; I'd best get along." As he passed Marcia, he made one last, brief eye contact with her. His eyes beamed at her with the exact same intensity as when he had uttered the words, "I wouldn't trust him."

Rob came back from letting the plumber out with a dumbfounded look on his face. "What are the chances we'd get a Canadian plumber?"

"Man, that was odd!" Marcia agreed. "I bet he's the only plumber in the U.S. who's ever even heard of Mary Ellen MacDonald."

"And he's the one we get."

"And how many plumbers have you heard throw around words like *somnambulistic*?"

"Well, I've never heard of one before. In fact, I've never heard anybody use that word before. You learn something every day, only I never thought I'd learn vocabulary words from a plumber." He grinned. "I guess that's what I get for judging a book by its overalls."

"And I'll say one other thing for him: he has the sharpest ears of anyone I've ever known. How did he overhear us from the kitchen? We were practically whispering."

"Maybe they get good ears from listening to the pipes."

Marcia got a terrible look in her eyes. "Do you think he overheard me describe the dream too? That part had to sound crazy."

"I wouldn't worry too much. I doubt he got enough context to have any idea what you were talking about. At worst, it must have sounded like you just had one odd dream."

"I guess so." She looked down at her plate. "I sure hope so."

They carried their breakfast plates around the corner. Rob turned on the faucet, opened the cabinet beneath, and inspected the pipes. "He does good work, too. I had this sink all bungled up and he fixed it in no time. We should make a note of his name in case we need plumbing work again—or if I need more vocabulary lessons."

"I'm not sure I want him back," Marcia said. "He seemed like a nice guy, but I'm freaked out enough these days without having the one guy in town who knows all about my crazy dreams here in the house."

Rob turned off the water and put his arm around her. "Yeah, I admit it's a little freaky, but he's from there. It's a crazy coincidence. What else could it be?"

The doorbell rang.

"You think our plumber thought of another ghost story?" Rob joked as he went to get the door.

There was another man dressed in overalls at the door when he opened it. This man looked very different from the last. In place of prim, this one was disheveled. The only similarity was that he wore the same type overalls with the same patch, advertising him as a representative of Capital Plumbing. The name on this man's patch was Butch.

Rob, in his confusion at seeing another plumber so soon, stared at the man without a word.

"Are you the guy who called about the broken sink?" Butch asked.

"Yeah. But somebody's already been here and fixed it."

Butch took a deep breath and rolled his eyes. "Look, Mac, if you want to call more than one plumber, fine. But the least you could do is call me off when the other company shows up. Now I drove all the way out here for nothing."

Rob held up his hand. "You don't understand. It was somebody from Capital Plumbing. That's the only place I called. They must have sent two of you over here by accident."

Butch squinted at him. "It's Saturday. I'm the only one out on residential calls today."

Rob shrugged. "I don't know what else to tell you. I called Capital Plumbing and a guy wearing a Capital Plumbing outfit showed up and fixed the sink. I'm sorry there was some confusion."

Butch chewed his lip, then asked, "You catch this other guy's name?"

"It said *Eli* on his patch."

Butch scowled. "We got no Eli at our shop."

"I swear, that's what the patch said."

Butch shook his head in disgust. "So, you don't want me to fix your sink?"

"No."

"Whatever," Butch said with a snort. "But we're still going to have to bill you for the house call."

Rob was in no shape to argue about bills. As Butch stomped back to his truck, Rob shut the door and shuffled back to the kitchen.

"Who was that?" Marcia asked.

Rob opened his mouth to tell her the amazing story. Then his mind caught up to it. "Uh, nothing. Just a college kid wanting to paint our house."

Chapter 15

Rob awoke to the smell of smoke. Leaning forward in the chair he'd been dozing in, he shook off sleep and attempted to claim his bearings. Everything around him was unusual, not only strange to him, but strange to his entire experience in the world. The room around him was small and square. It was made up entirely of straight lines and hard edges, not the least bit contemporary. Even the chair, upon which he slept, was sparsely upholstered with a coarse, ugly material.

Everything he saw seemed to be manufactured of wood or cast iron. There were some exceptions, his chair and another longer couch, the flimsy curtains covering the single rectangle of window, and oval rug on the floor. Except for the rug, the room was devoid of curves, just as it lacked the cushioning that made his home so comfortable to him. The spartan nature of this place made it alien and uninviting.

Even as he noted the foreignness of the room, his memory warmed to it. In some distant way, he knew this place. With each passing second, he knew it better, while the comforts and curves of his world receded into the background of his mind.

All these observations and latent memories came to him in an instant. The transition from unfamiliar to familiar happened in the blink of an eye. This was his parlor. He didn't have to consciously note it—who would consciously note waking within his own home?

In the next instant an instinct told him this strangely familiar world was threatened. The strong smell of smoke was not normal, even if Janet were stoking up the stove for supper. It was past supper anyhow. He, Janet, and Mary Ellen had all finished supper before his nap in the front room.

93

Alex bounded from his napping chair and followed the smell. He hadn't gone three steps when he heard a thud from the kitchen. He recalled that his daughter had begun studying in that room after supper. He called out to her. "Mary Ellen, you all right in there?"

No one answered.

He rushed toward the kitchen. When he reached it, his heart leapt into his throat. The room was on fire. Flames climbed up the wall opposite while Mary Ellen stood paralyzed, staring at the fire from the middle of the room.

Alex yanked the cloth from the table with a swift pull. Grabbing Mary Ellen by the arm, he dragged her catatonic body out of the way. He pitched into the fire with the tablecloth and all his might.

He doubted his ability to get the best of the fire with this flimsy tablecloth. Alex yelled his fear in words directed at Mary Ellen. "What have you done? What have you done?" The question was pointless. He gathered his strength and focused it all on the fire.

Regaining his composure helped him in the battle. His blows with the cloth began to tell aginst the flames. They receded down the wall until he was able to pound them to death against the floor. He stood up straight and caught his breath, surveying the charred wall. The damage there was disheartening enough, even without thinking of what it would have become if left unchecked for just a moment more.

These thoughts lit a new flame, this one within him. Alex tossed the cloth at the table and settled his gaze on Mary Ellen. Her eyes were full of tears, and he could tell she would run away from him if she weren't too scared to move. Buried far back inside Alex's consciousness, merely a helpless observer, Rob saw Mary Ellen's teary eyes—to him they were Emma's.

Alex pointed toward the outside door. "Go fetch me a switch!" he demanded of the girl.

Mary Ellen let out a cascade of sobs, shook her head in disbelief, and retreated a step or two. This was a not an instance when Alex would tolerate disobedience. His eyes narrowed as he strode a meaningful step toward her.

Mary Ellen took his meaning. She quit her retreat and stepped sideways past him to the door, passing through and letting it fall closed with a bang.

The slamming door brought Janet into the room. To Rob, buried where he could not participate, Janet's eyes were an older version of Marcia's. "What's all the commotion in here, Alex?" she asked him.

Alex stepped aside to give her a full view of the wall behind him. "Look here. That girl is up to her evil ways again. She nearly burned down the whole house, and with both her parents inside. Is this our reward for giving her a good home and loving parents?"

Janet covered her mouth and closed her eyes. "Dear Lord, Alex, what are we to do?"

"I'll tell you what I'll do, Janet. I'll whip her to within an inch of her life. And I'll do it over and over again until I chase The Devil out of her. That's what I'll do."

The door opened again and Mary Ellen squeezed through it. She looked up from the switch in her hand. Rob saw in her eyes the hope that at least the switch was adequate, and her choice of it wouldn't be held against her and added to the terms of her punishment.

"Give me that!" Alex snatched the switch from her. "I'm resolved to teach you the wickedness of your ways, girl, and one way or the other I *will* teach you."

He tested the flexibility of the switch in his hand for the benefit of Mary Ellen's terrified eyes.

"That's two fires inside a week. First you try to burn down the barn, with all my livestock in it, then you try to burn up your own parents in their own home. I don't even know what to say about it. Best I let this here switch do my talking."

Mary Ellen sidled toward her mother and addressed her appeal to the one whose heart still might be softened by her pleas. "No! I didn't do it! I swear, I didn't start them fires. I didn't do any of it. I

95

was just sleeping here at the table when something woke me up. The wall was already on fire when I woke!"

Janet stood still. There was a sign of melting in her eyes, but her body bent not the slightest.

Mary Ellen threw her arms around Janet's neck. "Oh, Ma! You got to believe me."

Alex stepped forward and tore the girl away from her mother. The well-trained farm wife tamped down her mother's instincts and let the girl be led away.

There was more room in the parlor. Alex pointed to a wood-framed chair. Mary Ellen dutifully moved it to the center of the room, making a last, desperate appeal for clemency with her eyes. Rob saw Emma's innocence in those eyes. He willed that his body would stop, but his will was not strong enough in this place. Alex controlled the limbs and Alex was unmoved in his anger.

Mary Ellen kneeled and bent over the chair. She wrapped one hand around a back dowel and the other around a leg. She squeezed tight her hands, her eyelids, and her jaw.

Alex was not one for ceremony. A man who enjoyed this might have dragged out the moment to build anticipation. A man who hated this might have delayed out of repulsion for this sort of thing. Alex neither loved nor hated it. He had no feeling for it at all. It was merely something that needed doing, like feeding the livestock. It was how children were disciplined, the only way he knew.

Rob hated it. He strained to hold the arms of the body he occupied. Failing that, he tried to close the eyes that would make him witness this, but Alex's eyes would not be closed to necessity.

Alex began at once. He swung the switch with a will, just like he did all his chores. He needed to hit hard for the blow to be properly felt through the material of Mary Ellen's long skirt. If the blow weren't properly felt, the task was not properly done, and the child would not benefit from the discipline. It was better to do it right than to do it often.

Mary Ellen cried out, though Rob could tell she tried to hold it in. He didn't want to be doing this to her. Even if he weren't in control, his perspective still made it as though he were beating her. Using every drop of willpower he owned, he still couldn't stop it. He couldn't walk away from it. He couldn't even turn his eyes away.

Rob burned to stop Alex's hand. The girl howled in pain, but Alex kept up the methodical pace of the strikes. She'd been punished enough. It was enough. For God's sake, enough!

Rob's shoulders vaulted forward. He found himself sitting up in his bed, panting for a long time before he could catch his breath. He took his head in his hands. His hair was soaked with sweat.

Chapter 16

Marcia sat up in bed beside Rob, laying her hand upon the back of his neck. "It's okay," she soothed. "It was a dream."

They stared into each other's faces while she waited for him to compose himself. "I was there," he said.

She rubbed the spot between his shoulders. "I know."

He looked askance at her. "How?"

"Did you look into Janet's eyes?"

"I looked where he looked. A few times at Janet, but mostly Mary Ellen. He was so intent on Mary Ellen."

"Did you see her in Mary Ellen's eyes?"

He winced. "Yes."

"We were all there together. I'm sorry you got dragged into it. But now that you are, we need to figure out what to do."

He gave her a quizzical look. "You're suddenly very calm about all this. I guess it's my turn to be the freaked-out one."

"It was your first time there. The first time is overwhelming. This time wasn't as shocking for me. It's like you get this feeling that somehow you belong there. It grows on you or something. Don't get me wrong; it's still weird as hell."

"Weird doesn't begin to describe it. Are these really dreams? And if not, what the hell are they?"

"I think this goes beyond all three of us having the same crazy dream. There's more to it than that. There's something we have to do, in this thing that seems half dream and half real."

"If it's not a dream, what could it possibly be? Where else do you go when you sleep?"

She shook her head once. "That's hard to say. Maybe it's some kind of vortex of unfinished business. I have no clue how we got involved, but—"

He squinted at her. "A vortex? You're pulling my leg now. We're not space travelers. We're not spiritual mediums. We're just normal people. What business would we have with a vortex?"

She took his hand in hers. "Yeah, it sounds crazy, but is it really that much crazier than three people having the same dream at the same time, and recognizing each other in the dream even though they are actually different people in the dream?"

"Right now, it all seems pretty crazy."

In the melting shadows of morning, they were distracted by a movement in the bedroom doorway. Emma's face peered shyly in at them.

"Come here, honey." Marcia said.

Emma tiptoed in, holding a wary stare for her father and giving him a wide berth as she made her way to her mother's side of the bed. Once there, she threw herself into her mother's waiting arms. "She didn't do it, Mommy! She really didn't!"

"I know, sweetheart. I know."

As Marcia rocked her in her arms, Emma let her eyes creep up toward Rob. "She really didn't," she whispered almost scornfully at him.

Rob leaned over and joined the hug. "Oh, sweetie, I'm so sorry. You know that wasn't really me, don't you? I could never do that to you, or her, or anybody. You know that, don't you?"

Emma's eyes softened. "I know," she whispered. "But it was so scary. I was so afraid."

Rob kissed her on the temple. "Emma, honey, I want you to know, you don't ever have to be afraid of me. I don't know what's going on in these dreams, but this is real life. I love you more than anything, and I would never hurt you, okay?"

"Okay."

Marcia took a deep breath. "Well, now that that's behind us, what are we going to do?"

"What can we do?" Rob asked.

"I'm getting the feeling that if we want these dreams, or whatever they are"—she threw a questioning look at her husband—"to go away, we have to do something to make them go away."

"What would you suggest?"

"I'm not sure. We've got to take control somehow. So far, we've been observers, but that has to change. We're there for a reason. We've got to find out what that is. If it's a good reason, we've got to see it through. If it's a bad reason, we've got to stop it."

"How would we know that?"

"I don't know. All I know at this moment is I don't like that Gatekeeper. Emma doesn't like him either. He's bad news."

"He's trying to drive Mary Ellen crazy," Emma added. "He wants everybody to think she's whacky."

"Did he ever say why he wants that?" Rob asked.

Emma shook her head. "I think he's just plain mean."

"That's another question I have," Rob continued. "Why didn't I see the Gatekeeper at all? Why didn't he come to get me like he did with you guys? I just popped right into the middle of the dream."

"He doesn't like grownups," Emma answered.

"What?"

"He told me the very first time I met him. He wanted me to bring you. I was supposed to get you to say you'd come. He said that was my duty. He doesn't like coming for grownups himself because they don't do their duty like kids do. They ask too many questions instead of just doing what they're told."

Marcia nodded. "They're harder to coerce."

"But he came for Mommy," Rob said.

"He came the first time, but not last night," Marcia answered. "Maybe he wanted to be sure I was willing the first time."

"And what about this portal of his in the stairs? That would have given more credence to your new theory, but without a physical doorway, it seems more like an actual dream than some alternate reality."

"Maybe he doesn't need the portal anymore." Marcia stopped speaking and drew in a quick breath.

She cast her eyes into one corner of the room and guided them across the ceiling to the far corner. "Or maybe the portal has grown," she whispered. "Maybe we've allowed him to build a far bigger doorway, without even realizing it."

"Allowed him? How?"

Marcia looked at him as if she were pointing out a tenant of basic logic. "We've both agreed to go. Before either of us went, we said out loud that we would go. He has the willing participation of the masters of the house."

Rob screwed his face up at her. "Where are you getting all this? Do you have some kind of folklore dictionary or something?"

"I don't know. It just sort of all makes sense to me. I don't know why, but I feel like it's all so plain all of a sudden."

"In that case, tell me this. Why does he want us all there so badly?" Rob asked.

"That, I don't know. It's what we've got to figure out. You think we could get ahold of that plumber again? I want to ask him some more questions."

Rob sighed. "I don't think that's going to happen."

"Let's just call his company again."

Rob gave a sardonic smile and puffed air out his nose. "He doesn't work there. He never did." He broke down and told her the truth about the second plumber coming to their door.

Chapter 17

Marcia went early to pick up Emma from preschool. Being home alone only encouraged her to obsess about the Gatekeeper and his other place. Parents were always welcome to sit in on preschool and the noise of children might be just the thing to distract her for a while.

When she arrived, the children were outside enjoying free play in the yard. Marcia spoke to one of the teachers for a while, then sat watching the children from the picnic table when the teacher went to supervise a distant group.

Emma noticed her mom and waved. Marcia waved back, which encouraged Emma to run to her mother's side. "What are you doing here?" Emma asked in her childish way of greeting.

"I just thought I'd come watch you for a while."

"Oh. Okay."

"Are you having a good day at school?"

"Yeah, I guess. But I just miss you."

Marcia smiled and put her arm around her little girl. "I miss you too."

They sat silently, enjoying the nearness to each other and watching the groups of children play.

Marcia started to relax for the first time all day. It felt like old times, snuggled up close to Emma like this. Maybe it was a sign. Maybe all the freaky stuff happening to them was about to pass away, leaving them a happy family again, no longer harassed by gatekeepers or dreams that might be more than dreams.

This is what a dream should be like, Marcia thought.

That thought was still fresh and new when Emma began to hum.

Marcia knew the melody by now. She knew it instantly. It woke her from her budding hopes.

"Emma, why do keep singing that song?" Marcia asked, trying to keep her tone even.

"I don't know. I kind of like it." Emma replied.

"I think it's creepy. I don't like it very much."

"I didn't either, when I heard the Gatekeeper sing it. But I liked it a lot better when I heard the lady play it on the Bluebird record. It sounded better then, and it seemed like it made her a little bit less sad."

"You mean the lady you told me about, who drank tea and looked at all those pictures?"

"Yeah. I think she liked that song a lot, and I felt sorry for her."

Marcia brushed the hair away from Emma's face. "Who do think that lady was?"

Emma hesitated, taking a deep breath. "Well, I think it was Mary Ellen, all grown up"—she looked away—"but it might have been me, too."

Marcia made a face that said she disagreed. "It was probably just Mary Ellen." It wasn't a total lie, but she wasn't sure she believed it was the total truth. "I wonder why you dreamed about her. Did the Gatekeeper say anything about her?"

"I don't think so. I try not to talk to him if I don't have to."

"Well, I guess that makes sense. And that dream does seem pretty tame next to the one about Mary Ellen lighting her house on fire."

Emma frowned at her. "Mommy, she didn't do it."

"You're right. I'm sorry. I know she didn't." Yet, it was easy for Marcia to assign blame to Mary Ellen. It made a complex situation simple to just assume Mary Ellen was behind it all. No wonder the people of her time accepted her guilt so readily. She was the easy answer.

Now, a hundred years later, Marcia would sell out Mary Ellen if it would put an end to her own troubles. If pinning blame on the girl meant these disturbing dreams would be over for her family, she'd heap on the blame with a will. But this long-ago girl was bound in some way to Emma, so she'd better be careful.

She rubbed Emma's back up and down. "I know she didn't do it, sweetie, I know."

"I'm glad."

They said no more as they sat close watching the other children play. In the sandbox, a little boy was making shapes with a pail. A larger boy took note of this and watched as the little boy grew more and more pleased with his work. At last, the big boy grabbed the arm of another small boy and pointed out the child in the sandbox to him. They watched and grinned at each other before approaching the sand box themselves.

As they approached the sandbox, the larger boy grinned a devious grin. Marcia could read his lips as he said, "Watch this," to his companion. He jumped into the sandbox and began trampling the shapes. When the creator of the shapes protested, he pushed the little child down. The little boy, knowing he was overmatched, ran away.

Marcia rose and stepped toward the box. Perhaps it would be better to inform the teacher than to interfere directly. She kept an eye on the sand box as she looked for the teacher. The big boy stepped out of the box. He made a motion toward the sand as if to indicate to his companion that it was free if he wanted to play in it now.

The second small boy was eager to attempt the shapes he had seen the first child make. He set to work eagerly. The large boy watched, happily noting his erstwhile companion's progress. When he was satisfied that enough time and care had been invested, he jumped into the box. To the other's disbelief, he treated the new shapes in the same fashion as the old. He showed more glee at destroying these creations than he had at crushing the first group.

Marcia came up to the teacher. She pointed toward the sandbox. As she opened her mouth to speak, it hit her.

She pushed the revelation to the side long enough to point out the trouble in the sand box to the teacher. Then she let it play in her mind as she walked back to Emma.

It all made sense. She didn't know exactly why it made sense, but it did. He was just like that bully in the sandbox. It was the same thing on a different level. Why it was important to know, she couldn't say, but it made her surer than ever that these dreams were not dreams at all.

She fidgeted at the picnic table with Emma until school was over, hardly paying any attention when the teacher came to thank her for helping to keep order in the yard. In the car, it was difficult to pay attention to the conversation Emma wanted to have. Too many thoughts were distracting her.

At home, she made Emma a quick snack, then found a private space to call Rob.

"He wants us to know!" she blurted before Rob was even done saying hello.

"Marcia? What are you talking about?"

"The Gatekeeper. He's taunting us!"

"Wait. What?"

"In these dreams—well, they're not dreams, but that's another issue. First, he let Emma watch him torture Mary Ellen. He even made her do stuff to Mary Ellen. Now, she's becoming Mary Ellen."

"I don't get it. What's the point?"

"Why would he show her? Why did he show me that Mary Ellen was adopted? If he wanted us in the roles of those people, why not just put us there to begin with? Why give us all this context? Why demonstrate to Emma that he's making Mary Ellen the scapegoat for all his troublemaking?"

"I don't know. Cause dreams are weird, and that's just the way they work sometimes?"

"He wants us to know all about it. It makes it worse for Emma, knowing how the fires started, and then being locked inside Mary

105

Ellen and not being able to do anything about it. It's all about making it harder for her to endure. For us too."

Rob hemmed and hawed at the other end of the line. "I don't know, honey. Maybe we're overthinking all of this. I know I was in rough shape this morning, but in the light of day, things look different."

"Maybe to you, but I'm more convinced than ever we need to take this seriously. Listen. Remember Emma told us she had another dream that she was a full-grown woman? The one who drank tea and listened to music, and was just so sad the whole time?"

"How's that play into this?" he asked.

"He wants her to know what's in store for her. He wants her to see the misery he's going to cause. And that song she heard in the dream. I half think he wanted us to use that as the thread to learn about the whole MacDonald story. He wants us to know exactly what he's doing, because he's about to do it to us."

"But why?"

"I don't know. Maybe he's just one sadistic bastard, or maybe he's trying to wear us down, so we'll be less able to resist." A sob escaped her. "Rob, I don't want to go to sleep again."

"Babe, we've got to sleep."

Chapter 18

They didn't get many automobiles coming out to the farm. Alex made out the distinct sound of the approaching vehicle from inside the house. He pulled the curtain back from the window and watched the black coupe climb up the hill. There was a new dusting of snow over the dirt road, but the old snow was packed, so the car had little trouble making it up.

The auto's flexible bonnet was pulled up, covering the cockpit. Alex couldn't tell who was inside. Still, he figured it must have been something important to drive all the way out from town. He had an idea of who it might be, but he would let things play out without jumping to conclusions. He was too practical to get ahead of himself with anticipation.

The automobile came to a stop beside the house. The passenger door opened and a man in a dark suit and hat emerged. He reached in behind him to extract a suitcase, saying some parting words to the driver. He closed the door and gave a little wave goodbye. As the car turned around and drove away, he looked up and surveyed the house in front of him, just the way a stranger would do in a new environment. Having taken it all in, he came to the door.

The visitor's frame was narrow at the shoulders and at his legs, but with a round section between. He wore a confident mien as he took in his new surroundings, like a man who was already drawing important conclusions out of the very air around him.

Alex let him knock before opening the door. That was the proper order of things. Besides, Alex was not altogether eager to meet the man.

The man looked up at Alex with clear, sympathetic eyes. "Mr. MacDonald? How do you do, sir? I'm Dr. Prince."

Alex nodded and stepped to the side. "We didn't know when to expect you," he said.

Dr. Prince chuckled away Alex's awkward greeting. "Well, that's the way it is when one gets off the beaten path like this. I wasn't sure myself how I would find my way here. Fortunately, I was able to beg a lift from one of the men in town. Nice folks, way out here. I'll give you that."

The doctor took advantage of the path Alex had allowed to step into the house, taking off his hat to reveal greying hair, cropped short at the sides and combed back on top. "Where would you like me to put this?" he asked raising up his suitcase.

"I'll get Mary Ellen to clear out of her room. You can bunk there. She'll sleep with us."

"In the meantime, might I set it down here?" the doctor asked. "It gets rather heavy after a while."

"You might as well."

"And my hat and coat?"

Alex took them and hung them on a board. "I'll call Mary Ellen down."

Dr. Prince put a hand on his arm. "If you don't mind, I'd like to talk to you first. Maybe Mary Ellen could prepare the room in the meantime. I'd hoped to speak to you, and maybe Mrs. MacDonald, before we brought Mary Ellen into this."

"Mrs. MacDonald is sick to bed."

Dr. Prince's eyes lit with compassion. "Ah, that's too bad. I hope it's nothing serious."

"She gets headaches. Done it for years."

"That's a relief to know. I suppose it's just us then." Dr. Prince took the liberty of a seat. Alex meant to follow, but the doctor interrupted. "Perhaps the young lady could get started on the room?" he prompted as he lifted his eyebrows toward the upstairs.

Alex went to the foot of the steps and yelled up. "Mary Ellen!"

The girl's voice came back. "Yes, Pa?"

"We have company. Bring your things down to put in with Ma and me. Then make up the bed with fresh linen."

"Yes, Pa."

"A very agreeable girl," Dr. Prince commented as Alex returned to the parlor.

"She has been. She's been a right good girl, most all along"—he took a seat beside the doctor—"up 'til lately."

Dr. Prince issued a warm smile with his soft eyes. "Yes. That's what makes situations like these so difficult. It's not easy for parents to watch their good children become so troubled."

"You think it's all her doing, then? The fires?"

"That's what I've come to discover. But let me ask you, is there a logical alternative?"

Alex pursed his lips and shook his head. "Not to my mind. Mary Ellen claims she didn't do any of it at all, but when she's the only one around, what can I think?"

Dr. Prince nodded. "Indeed. What choice do you have?"

Alex went on. "She says it's some sort of ghost that's doing it. Says she's sensed him a few times. But I can't put stock in no ghost."

"Nor should you. The answer to this question is the logical one. It always is. That will be proved soon enough. Our true task will be to discover the reason why things have taken the turn they have. Only then do we have any hope of remedying the situation."

"Sounds like you're already convinced Mary Ellen's behind it all."

Dr. Prince locked his eyes with Alex's. "Like you, I am a man of good sense. From everything I know of this case, good sense leads to only one conclusion. Nothing will be solved if you abandon your better judgment. That's my opening advice to you."

Alex sighed. "I was half hoping you'd advise me to believe in ghosts."

"As much as I would like to provide you an alternative culprit, I'm afraid that would be malpractice. We must attack this problem as people of reason."

Alex gazed into the healing eyes of Dr. Prince. "What would you have us do?"

Dr. Prince was distracted by the sound of footfalls making their way down the stairs at a deliberate pace. Instead of answering Alex, he watched the foot of the stairs until Mary Ellen appeared, her arms loaded with bedding.

At the sight of her, Dr. Prince's eyebrows raised, almost in a sort of delight. "That's Mary Ellen." Alex supposed Dr. Prince meant it as a question, even though it sounded more like a self-satisfied statement.

"That's her," Alex answered, assuming the doctor had asked him. He turned to command his daughter. "Take those things in with your Ma. Then come back here. We have a visitor."

"Yes, Pa," she answered before disappearing around the corner.

"She'll be back, directly," Alex assured his guest.

"I look forward to our meeting," Dr. Prince replied, still staring at the place where Mary Ellen had been.

Having delivered her load to her parents' bedroom, she returned. "Come here and pay respects to Dr. Prince," her father said.

She stopped in front of the place where they sat and performed a shy curtsy toward the guest.

"How do you do, Mary Ellen?" the guest asked. "I'm Dr. Prince. I've come to help you with this business of the fires."

The girl fought off a blush. "How do you do, Dr. Prince?" she said in a meek voice.

The doctor's lips curled up at the corners. "I think we'll both do fine together, Mary Ellen." He leaned forward and examined her face. "I think we'll do just fine indeed."

Deep in the back of Mary Ellen's mind, there was a jolt. It was not enough to move her or make her speak out, but there was a revelation. The revelation occurred in the part of her that was Emma.

The helpless witness, Emma, saw a familiar pair of eyes in this newcomer. Though hidden beneath the makeup of sympathy and compassion, she saw eyes that had heretofore shown neither of those attributes. They had only shown taunting cruelty. There could be no doubt they were the same eyes.

Emma yearned to speak out, to warn Alex of the danger in their midst, but she was a captive in Mary Ellen's presence. She could no more move Mary Ellen's tongue to speak than she could move Mary Ellen's legs to run away. Alex would not understand the warning anyway, but her father would. It was hopeless to try to warn him now. But when they were all awake again, it would be a different story. If nothing terrible happened before they woke up, everything might yet be all right.

Dr. Prince turned to Alex. "It would be most helpful to my investigation if I could speak to the child alone. Would you mind leaving us for a moment or two?"

Mary Ellen's body tensed, but that was all she would do on her own, and Emma could do nothing to make her demonstrate more resistance to the request.

Alex rose. "I'll go feed the livestock." At the door he turned back to his daughter. "You pay close attention to what the doctor tells you, Mary Ellen. He's here to help you."

As Mary Ellen watched her father go out, Dr. Prince leaned forward and grabbed her by the arms. His touch was gentle, almost friendly, but its unexpectedness made Mary Ellen flinch. He had gotten her attention. "Hello there, Mary Ellen," he said in voice that was too soft and sweet by half.

"Hello," she said, stifling the impulse to break his grip. His clear, blue eyes were the kind that embarrassed the innocent by making them think he could see through their souls.

"Now let's get something straight, from the top," he said, putting an edge to his sweet voice with the way he carefully pronounced the words. "You can't outwit me."

Mary Ellen stared at him in confusion, but he was no longer speaking to her. He drew her closer and stared into her eyes with his own piercing vision. "You. The little girl inside," he whispered. "You recognize me. Of course you do. And there's nothing you can do about it. You can't warn them, can you? You can't make this daft girl do anything, can you?" He shook Mary Ellen's frame. "You're helpless in there, aren't you?"

Mary Ellen tried to pull away, but Dr. Prince only tightened his grip and chuckled. "Ah, but you're a clever one though, aren't you? I bet you've already figured out how you will go running to tell them the minute you wake up in your own world." He shook his head and tisked her. "Such a pity that will never happen."

All at once his face became serious and he pulled Mary Ellen very near. "Listen to me," he said into Mary Ellen's eyes. "The best thing for you is to do whatever I tell you. I have something for you to do for me." His look softened. "But that can wait a while. For now, all that matters is that we understand each other. And even if you don't truly understand me now, you will soon enough."

He released his grip on Mary Ellen and brushed away the crinkles in her sleeves with his hands. Resuming his sweet voice, he told her, "There now, Mary Ellen, don't look so fearful. I'm not an ogre, after all. I'm here to help you. Now, sit down and let us chat."

He guided her into the seat her father had vacated. "That's good, Mary Ellen. Now that you're comfortable, why don't you tell me about all these fires you've been lighting over the past couple of months."

Chapter 19

Emma knew she was lying in her bed. She sensed the growing light within her room. It was morning and the natural thing to do would be to open her eyes and sit up. She could do neither of these things.

Her head hurt and she felt unusually tired. She was cold to the point of shivering. She wanted another blanket, but she was helpless to get one. Not being able to move or open her eyes was frightening. She called out for her mother, but accomplished little more than a low moan, since she could not move her lips. A wave of panic swept over her, but she had not the energy to maintain it and it quickly melted away into the numbness of her being.

Of all the things she could normally do without effort, the one she could do best now was hear. She heard someone come in. Her name was being called. Her mother was telling her it was time to get up. She couldn't answer. All she managed was another soft moan.

Her mother came near. She was being shaken, gently at first, but more vigorously every moment. The shaking hurt. She tried to say so, but the words were lost in her throat.

Her mother's voice asked what was the matter, why wouldn't she wake up?

A hand felt her forehead. The voice told her she was burning up. The voice got louder. Her mother was calling out to her father. The voice sounded scared, and that was scary to hear.

The sound of more footsteps entered the room. Her father's voice asked what was happening. Her mother's frantic voice said alarming things to him. Her father's strong hands cupped her shoulders. There was more shaking. It hurt worse than before. He was talking to her. She mustered a faint moan in reply.

Her mother mentioned the hospital. Emma hated the hospital. It was a frightening place, and if you went there it meant you were really sick. She heard the word ambulance. That was worse. She had only known one person to be taken in an ambulance, and he died. It didn't matter that he was very old; people who rode in ambulances were sick enough to die. But she was becoming too tired to worry. The voices, no less alarmed, grew faint.

When the voices returned, she was not in her own bed. This bed was unfamiliar. It smelled funny. It didn't smell like a bed for kids.

There were three voices now. Her mother's voice and her father's voice shot out questions, one after another. The third voice tried to answer them all, but it said, "We don't know yet," more than it said anything else.

There was a familiar tone in her parents' voices. It was just like the one she heard from them when she was trying to talk her way out of a bath. They always said they didn't have time to talk in circles with her when she acted like that. It must be that the other voice was talking in circles to them.

She wished she could make them feel better. She would gladly have a bath right now if it would make them happy. She wouldn't talk in circles to them, if only she could talk at all.

But she couldn't talk, and for now, she couldn't even stay awake.

Chapter 20

Mary Ellen stared at Dr. Prince. She knew he'd asked her a question, but it seemed like hours had intervened since then. She couldn't even remember what he had asked her.

"You don't want to answer me?" he asked. "Well, that's okay. It just so happens that I know why you like starting fires. You like starting fires because it's your duty. Your parents are bad people." His eyes grew wide and his lips animated. "They are evil, and evil must be stopped."

Mary Ellen attempted to back away from him, but he held her arms. "Don't be frightened, Mary Ellen. It's okay. I'll guide you. We've been through this all before. You don't remember, but we've been through it. We lived it all, but without achieving our goals. This time, we will succeed. We were foolish, you and I, to rely on fire. Fire is such an unreliable weapon. This time we will be surer of ourselves. Look."

The doctor let go of her with one hand and reached into his jacket pocket. When the hand came back into view it was holding a revolver. Mary Ellen lurched, but one hand was enough to hold her. "Don't be alarmed. It's a very simple device. All you have to do is pull back this hammer, point, and squeeze the trigger. But I don't have to show you, do I? A country girl like you knows all about shooting."

Mary Ellen shook her head and strained against his grasp. "No. No."

Dr. Prince yanked her toward him. "Let me tell you a little secret."

Replacing the revolver in his pocket, he used his empty hand to guide her head near to his. He placed his lips next to her ear and whispered, "Hello in there, Emma. I'm talking to you now. Do you remember all the things I told you about your duty? Well, this is where you perform your duty. Mary Ellen is a failure. The last time she lived this life, she showed she can't do what needs to be done. That's why I chose you to help her. You are a little girl of courage. You can do what needs to be done. You must guide poor, helpless Mary Ellen now. I give you the power to do so."

Emma felt a wave of new energy. She could move Mary Ellen's limbs. No longer only seeing the world through Mary Ellen's eyes, she could direct Mary Ellen's eyes where she would. She controlled Mary Ellen's tongue. "Why are you doing this?" she asked with Mary Ellen's mouth.

He chuckled into her ear. "Dear child, I'm doing this because this is what I do. We all serve a master who instructs us to our duty. My master instructs me to do as I do, and I, your master, lay your duty before you."

"I won't shoot people," Emma told him. "Only bad people shoot other people."

"Oh, but when the people are bad, it takes a good girl to shoot them. And you know Mary Ellen's parents are bad people. You saw how her father whipped her for starting fires she never even started. He wouldn't even let her explain herself. Does a good father do that? Would your father do that?"

Emma was sure he wouldn't, but she didn't say anything.

"And her mother just stood there like a bump on a log and let him do it. She didn't even try to save her own daughter. Is that a good a person? Would your mother treat you that way?"

"I still won't shoot them," Emma insisted.

"But think of Mary Ellen," he went on. "They'll end up putting her in the crazy house. You don't want that, do you? She's such a nice girl, so sweet and innocent. But once she goes to the crazy house, that's that for her."

He wiped his palms across each other as if making an end to the story.

"You saw how miserable her life will be if that happens. Even when they let her out again, she'll be alone, with not a single friend in the world. Don't you remember looking at the book of clippings? She'll never get over it. Her life is ruined. Unless. . ." He invited her to follow his eyes toward the pocket holding the revolver.

Emma stomped Mary Ellen's foot on the floor. "I won't. I won't do bad things just because you tell me to. I don't even really know you."

He chuckled at her. "Of course you do, my dear. You've sung my praises with that sweet little voice of yours. I'm the Little Man Who Wasn't There."

"That's right," Emma scoffed. "You're not there. This is just a bad dream."

Dr. Prince shrugged with his face. "Perhaps you are right. This is just a dream. Well then, don't you think it would end sooner if you just did what you're supposed to do? And what difference would it make after you woke up? You didn't really shoot anybody. It was all just a dream. So why not do what I ask and be done with it?"

"I can't."

"Why not? Why not put an end to all this?"

"Because."

Emma couldn't explain it, even to herself. If she were going to be a good girl, she had to be good all the time, even in dreams. She couldn't tell why, but she knew this was true. She shouldn't do bad things just because she could get away with it. And then, there had always been something about these visits that felt like more than a dream. Maybe it was just a more real-feeling dream, or maybe it was something else. Even if it were just a dream, she saw her own mother and father in the eyes of Mary Ellen's parents, and for this alone, she could never hurt them.

"Because what?"

"Just because, that's all. If you want to shoot them, go ahead. Do it yourself. But I won't do it for you."

Dr. Prince smirked. "Yes, I could shoot them myself, but that wouldn't have quite the same impact, would it?"

"I don't know what you're talking about."

The doctor shrugged. "That's true. You don't. So let me tell you. These fires and pranks have been good fun, but it's time to take this game to the next level. Mary Ellen disappointed me last time, but you won't disappoint me this time, will you? No. Of course you won't. I won't be disappointed again. I've waited a century for this chance, and I won't let you ruin it."

Emma shied away from him. "I won't ruin anything. Just let me go back to my real life and leave me alone."

Dr. Prince blinked a slow blink and shook his head. "I can't do that, my child. You see, it's taken me years to find you. Do you have any idea how difficult it is to find a family that perfectly matches this one? Physical appearance is one thing, but then you all needed precisely the right light behind your eyes. You are my needle in the haystack, and you will succeed where Mary Ellen has failed. You must. I will not go sifting through haystacks for another hundred years."

"I don't understand any of this!" Emma groaned.

Dr. Prince curled his upper lip to show his top row of teeth. "And that is precisely why I am taking such pains to explain it to you. Because your family's well-being depends upon you knowing just what you have to do."

He blinked and exhaled a deep breath of disappointment before explaining further.

"You see, this is sort of a do-over. Mary Ellen had a job to do, once upon a time, and she failed. She was too feeble-minded to see it through. Her failure gave me a displeasing hue in the eyes of my master. Consequently, I was condemned to roam the world until I could find a family to reenact her little drama and bring it to a satisfactory conclusion the next time around. They had to be just right, and have a girl with the pluck to see things through to the end. I found you. And now that the three of you have all agreed to join in your roles, the drama will commence. I wish I could have waited until you were older, but that was not possible."

"Why not?" Emma asked before realizing she didn't care why not.

"Because you will only be the perfect family for a few months more." The doctor's face flashed anger. "This baby boy inside your mother pushes us to act quickly."

Mary Ellen's eyes widened with Emma's surprise. "How did you know about the baby?"

"Don't you remember? You told me."

Emma remembered telling the Gatekeeper, only it was hard to always keep in mind that he was the one behind this disguise.

"But I knew before that." Dr. Prince stared in disgust. "I knew about him before any of you. That is why I had to come to you before I wished to."

"How did you know before anybody else?"

"I knew because I know things!" he shouted. "What difference does it make? What matters is that the clock is ticking. You will do your duty before it winds out, or I will have to take measures to remove the deadline altogether."

Chapter 21

"This is insane!" Marcia's frustration broke the uneasy silence. "They've been running tests all day. Why can't they tell us what's wrong with her?"

Rob put his arm around her. "Hey, it'll be okay. Look at the bright side. They've got her fever down, and she's not writhing in pain or anything. They'll figure it out. And she's a tough kid. She'll come through this all right."

They sat on the floor with their backs to the wall, facing their daughter's hospital bed. It was night and the lights were off, but they could see Emma's face in the glow of her monitor.

The nurses had brought them pillows and blankets, which they had spread out around them, the chairs in the room not being suitable for rest. Marcia hugged one of the pillows. "If she has some sort of infection, don't you think they should have found out what was causing it by now? They should have found it by now, shouldn't they?"

"I don't know. Maybe some infections are more complicated than others."

Marcia pressed her face into the pillow and then pulled it out again. "Oh God, you don't think something's attacking her brain, do you?"

Rob tried to look confident. "No. That doesn't seem right. I think she'd be thrashing around or something in that case." He worked up a weak chuckle. "They'll probably figure out it's some dumb thing like Mono in the morning."

Marcia didn't believe that. She doubted he believed it. She drew up her knees and set the pillow on them so she could rest her head. She stared at Rob for a while, trying to read his thoughts through his face. "You don't think …" She stopped to consider the depth of her thought. "You don't think this has anything to do with the dreams?"

"You mean the not-dreams? To tell you the truth, I was just wondering that myself."

"I don't want to face those again. Not now. Not with my little girl so vulnerable. Rob, I'm afraid to go to sleep."

He took her hand. "What if this is related to that? Then, maybe the best place to help her is from that other place. Maybe we're wasting time staying awake here."

"You think so? But how could we help her? We can't control anything there. We're helpless observers."

"Yeah, but we've got to try to do something. She could be trapped there right now. We can't do much for her here. At the very least, maybe we can learn something that will help if we go there. It's something."

Marcia stretched herself out on the blankets. Her face showed fear, but also determination. "Okay. Lie down with me, and let's go see if there's something we can do for our little girl."

Chapter 22

Alex forked out hay to the livestock as Dr. Prince appeared in the doorway. "So this is the barn," the doctor said as a greeting. "The place where all the mischief began."

Alex leaned on the handle of his pitchfork. "Yeah. This is it."

Dr. Prince stepped in out of the bright but cold day. "Switching livestock in their pens and braiding their tails, is that right?"

Alex nodded. "That's how it all began."

"All that must seem rather harmless now."

"It's a far sight less trouble than fires."

Dr. Prince talked over his own shoulder as he walked along, giving himself a tour of the stalls. "Indeed. These fires push the concept of childish pranks a bit too far."

Alex stared at him with a grim face. "That they do."

Satisfied with his inspection, the doctor turned back toward Alex. "I've had a nice little conversation with Mary Ellen. It was very enlightening. I've concluded that she is indeed responsible for these fires."

Alex had all he could do to refrain from rolling his eyes at the learned investigator. "We figured that. Weren't nobody else who *could* be responsible. She'll swear up and down she didn't do it, but who else could have?"

Dr. Prince looked at him squarely with his soft, reasonable eyes. "Of course. We've been over that before. I just wanted you to know that my discussion with Mary Ellen has confirmed my suspicions. Didn't want you to think I'd drawn conclusions before speaking to her."

Alex looked away. "So now you're sure of it. I'm sorry if I don't seem happy about it."

Dr. Prince touched him on the forearm. "Why should you? I'm only confirming what you've known all along. But I also know there has always been a hopeful part of you that wished there could be some other explanation—something that hadn't occurred to you—something that could exonerate Mary Ellen and still make sense to a practical man."

Alex squinted. "It was a foolish hope."

The doctor climbed two steps up the ladder toward the loft, reached up, and pulled a handful of straw loose from a bale resting there. He stepped down and twisted the bundle into a little knot. His expression brightened. "Perhaps not totally."

Alex raised his eyebrows. "How's that?"

"She may not be conscious that she's doing it. It may be that she slips into some state wherein she is not herself. This is well-documented in psychological research. Some think people in these states are under the influence of a spirit guide, but I believe there is a more natural explanation."

"Such as?"

"Abnormal functioning of the brain. Some people have multiple personalities. I believe that a portion of these go undetected because the latent personality does not show itself to other people. It may not even be a wholly separate personality. It might be just enough different that it acts out of character for Mary Ellen and does not then allow her any memory of the act."

Alex's head hung down. "She's crazy?"

"I don't think so. I think she's a fairly normal child who is subject to periodic bouts of abnormal brain function. With your help, I think we can fix that."

His head still bowed, Alex gave a sorrowful nod.

"Are you committed to helping her?" Dr. Prince twisted the little knot of straw tight with both hands. "Because she desperately needs your help."

Alex raised his head. A tear ran down his cheek. "Yes. I'll do anything."

Dr. Prince looked at Alex sideways. "It may not be easy for you. Getting the message through to that latent personality will not be a pleasant task. Nonetheless, it's the only way." Having finished saying all he wished, he exaggerated a shiver under his overcoat. "It's too cold for my bones in this barn. If you don't mind, I'm going back into the house. It's slightly warmer there."

Alex made no objection.

"By the way"—the doctor glanced back over his shoulder—"Mrs. MacDonald is up and around. I introduced myself to her before I came out. I'm very glad she's feeling better."

Alex nodded and the doctor disappeared into the winter sunshine. Though the doctor seemed genuinely determined to help them, Alex was not sorry to be left alone. Dr. Prince liked to talk more than Alex did, especially when he had weighty matters on his mind. Thinking was best done alone.

Alex moved hay around with his pitchfork to no purpose. His mind had abandoned the execution of his chores. It was centered upon what Dr. Prince had said.

Maybe Mary Ellen wasn't crazy, but the doctor had certainly called her abnormal. That wasn't a nice thing to have your daughter called. What exactly it meant was unclear to him, but it wasn't good. That much he knew.

It hurt. Alex had hoped Dr. Prince would find some answer he hadn't thought of, maybe some weird quirk of science he was too uneducated to know—anything that gave him his little girl back. Instead, Dr. Prince had confirmed his worst fear: something was wrong with Mary Ellen. Her mind wasn't right. He could never run away from Mary Ellen like he could from science beyond his comprehension, or even ghosts.

Alex pondered worrying questions. Where would this all lead? To the asylum? He was no expert, but he didn't remember any cases of people with brain sicknesses ever getting cured. This little girl who had come into his barren life and given him a family was precious. He wasn't always good at showing it, but this little girl—his little girl—was the apple of his eye. The thought of Mary Ellen wasting away in a mental institution made him want to vomit. He would almost rather see her dead.

All the doctor's words about unconscious states confused him. If Mary Ellen wasn't Mary Ellen all the time, Alex wanted to know, then who else was she? He couldn't imagine how one person could have two personalities that didn't even know what each other were doing. It made no sense, and if something made no sense, he was not likely to understand it.

Rob, who was privy to all these thoughts, shared Alex's confusion. He understood Mary Ellen wasn't starting any fires. On the other hand, he knew there was another consciousness operating inside her. What he didn't get is why it had to be Emma.

Chapter 23

Janet swept her broom over the parlor floor. It was unfortunate that Dr. Prince had arrived from the United States when she was feeling ill. She hadn't the chance to make their home as presentable as she would have liked. Yes, they were modest, country folk, and they didn't have as many fancy embellishments around their home as a city doctor might be accustomed to, but what little they did have was kept neat and tidy.

The door opened and Dr. Prince came in from the cold. As he shook the chill off his bones, he smiled with his soft, grandfatherly eyes.

Janet leaned her broom on a chair and went to the doctor. She stepped behind him and held up her hands. "Let me take your coat for you."

"I'm almost tempted to keep it on in this frigid weather," he said, letting her help him shed his overcoat and handing her his hat as well.

She hung his things on a peg. "I'll build up the fire if you like. Alex doesn't like to burn too much wood in the daytime, but seeing as we have a guest, I guess it would be all right."

"Don't go to the trouble on my account. Besides, I'd like to get settled into my room. Mr. MacDonald indicated there was a room upstairs at my disposal."

Janet's face drooped. "Mary Ellen's room." She spoke through a layer of embarrassment. "You must forgive me doctor, but as I was feeling poorly, I hadn't the chance to freshen the room up for you. Children can be so forgetful about tidiness, you see." She pointed to the most comfortable chair she owned. "If you'd be so kind as to sit here for a moment, I'll go up and make sure the room is suitable to welcome such an honored guest."

"Perhaps that's best," he said. "I confess I'd hardly know what to do with a child's things if I found them in my way."

Having bought herself a little time, Janet rushed upstairs and began a whirlwind straightening of her daughter's room. She'd hardly made any headway when she smelled smoke. A walk to the head of the stairs convinced her the odor rose from the floor below.

Rushing down the stairs, she crossed the parlor and was drawn toward the pantry by the smell. At the pantry door, she found that Dr. Prince had proceeded her by a few steps.

"It's coming from here," he told her. He threw open the door to reveal a wall of flame consuming the shelves and the dry goods thereupon. "Get me something to beat it down!"

Janet dashed off and brought back a blanket.

Dr. prince grabbed the blanket and beat the flames. "Get your husband! And any buckets he has in the barn!"

Janet turned to go and nearly tripped over Mary Ellen, who was standing beyond the doorway, staring into the pantry in horror and confusion.

For a second, Janet stopped and searched Mary Ellen's eyes, looking for that first instant of unguarded expression, to see if there were a confession or a protest of innocence in that fleeting glimpse of truth.

In Mary Ellen's eyes, Marcia saw Emma. Emma held no question of Mary Ellen's innocence. The familiar eyes that shone through from within Mary Ellen's confirmed her certainty. Marcia embraced that certainty with all her heart.

Janet lingered. The only truth she found in Mary Ellen's eyes was her daughter's fearfulness. Yet, from somewhere inside her came a small wave of hope for Mary Ellen's innocence.

"Go! Quickly!" Dr. Prince prodded Janet as he waged single combat against the flames.

Janet pushed past her daughter and ran out of the house.

Alex was in the barn when he heard her yelling his name. He dashed out to meet her halfway.

"Fire! Fire in the house!" she wailed. "Bring a bucket!"

Alex hurried back for a bucket and snatched a nearby horse blanket as well. When he got to the house, Janet was already inside. He tossed the bucket at her and joined Dr. Prince in beating at the flames with his blanket.

Mary Ellen helped her mother fill the bucket at the kitchen pump. Janet ferried the bucket to the men in the pantry. With the help of water and blankets, the men put out the fire. Then they emerged to consider Mary Ellen.

Mary Ellen didn't speak. She had learned that attempting to declare her innocence only made matters worse for her. Her eyes seemed to surrender all hope of avoiding blame.

Alex was held in limbo by the doctor's presence. It would not do to go on scowling at Mary Ellen without taking some action, so he turned his eyes toward Dr. Prince, looking for guidance.

Dr. Prince read Alex's expression. He turned to Janet. "Stay here with the girl while I talk things over with your husband."

He led Alex into the next room. When the women were out of earshot, he said, "You must be very forceful with her."

"I have been," Alex replied. "I've whipped her after every fire, but it does her no good."

Dr. Prince responded in a quiet voice that was as soft as his grandfatherly eyes. "Then you must whip her harder, longer. You must get through to her by main force."

Alex knit his brow. "But you told me she doesn't even know what she's doing."

Dr. Prince nodded. "That is quite probable, which is exactly why you must be resolute. You must get through to her subconscious. You can't do that with a mere slap on the wrist."

Alex pulled his lips tight against his teeth. "It doesn't seem right. If she's not in her right mind."

"You must not let your judgment be clouded by your ideas of fairness." Dr. Prince raised his hand and pointed his finger upward to accentuate his instructions. "You must stay committed to helping her. You can't help her by letting this behavior continue. You must punish her so that whatever other personality dwells within her is also awakened to the consequences of her wayward actions. She'll thank you when it's all said and done."

"Are you sure?" Alex asked.

"I've never been more certain. The child craves correction. She wants the troublemaking personality chastised more than anything. She's crying out for your help against it. But the longer you wait, the less effective it will be."

"I'll have her fetch a switch."

Alex turned to go back to the women, but Dr. Prince caught him by the arm. "A switch will hardly answer this case. I have just the thing you need. I'll be right back."

Dr. Prince trotted almost gleefully to his baggage, leaving Alex to ponder darkly over what form of punishment his guest might be storing in his luggage. Alex did not have long to wonder. Dr. Prince returned directly, striding triumphantly with a knotted cane in his hand.

Alex frowned and took an unconscious step backward.

The Doctor's eyes beamed as if he had retrieved a great and treasured artifact. "Rattan!" He said the word with the emphasis of a world-altering revelation. "The switch hasn't yet grown that could half measure up to the rattan cane for such work as you have." He thrust the cane at Alex.

Alex flinched as though he were expecting the punishment himself, making no effort to take the cane.

The doctor thrust it at Alex with more enthusiasm. "Remember, no half measures. This should make some headway against her subconscious."

Alex looked askance at the doctor. Even for a no-nonsense fellow, this was a stern punishment.

Seeing it all through Alex, Rob clenched his entire consciousness against the very idea of the cane. It was a cruel punishment for any child, but especially for a child who held his very own Emma within her eyes. What effect his consciousness would have on Alex was uncertain, but Rob feared it would not be enough.

"I understand your reluctance," Dr. Prince said in a velvet tone. "But it's for the best. You simply must get through to her before someone labels her insane. Then you would certainly lose her."

Alex sighed and accepted the cane. The doctor's bearing was so confident and his eyes so reassuring that Alex could scarcely doubt he knew his business. Besides, experience had shown that Alex was not competent to solve this problem by himself.

Dr. Prince was a convincing speaker. Though Rob raged with all his will against the idea of the rattan cane, he found himself no match for the smooth persuasions of the doctor in guiding Alex's actions. Cane in hand, Alex moved step by step against Rob's will.

Dr. Prince walked a step behind Alex, to reinforce him, as they returned to where they had left the womenfolk. When Janet saw the cane she gasped aloud. Mary Ellen began to shake.

The girl caught hold of her mother's waist as she hid herself behind the woman. She cried out to anyone who might believe her. "No! I didn't do it! I wasn't even in the pantry!"

Alex stopped short. "Did you see her in the pantry?" he asked his wife.

Janet answered with a clear, quick, "No." She shook her head just as clearly. "When Dr. Prince and I got here there was no one inside."

Alex relaxed his grip on the cane.

Dr. Prince frowned. "I saw her. I was ahead of Mrs. MacDonald getting here. I was just in time to see her sneak out and run around the corner. Of course, Mrs. MacDonald wasn't in any position to see, but I was."

Emma tested her ability to control Mary Ellen by making her speak. "He's lying! Mary Ellen never went near the pantry!"

Dr. Prince gave Alex a meaningful stare. "Do you hear that? The devil within rises toward the surface. Now is the time to strike at it!"

The doctor's words stiffened Alex. He stepped around Janet and reached for his daughter.

Emma learned a lesson. Making Mary Ellen say things without thinking them through was worse than not being able to make her speak at all.

Tears flowed down Janet's face. She was held in place by the testimony of the doctor and the resolve of her husband. She offered no resistance.

From within, Marcia screamed mute passion. No matter the doctor. No matter the husband. This was her daughter. There was no reason on Earth to let them do this to her. If there were ever a time to stand firm in one's love for her child, this was that time.

Alex tugged Mary Ellen from her mother.

Janet slumped into helpless tears.

Marcia raged desperately against the scene, chanting mental encouragements to Janet, imploring the woman with every motherly emotion to protect her daughter.

As Alex dragged her away, Mary Ellen's hopeless eyes sought out her mother's face. Janet fought the urge to look away. Because, more than anything else, she was this child's mother, she defeated the urge. Reinforced by the spirit of another mother within her, bolstering her natural instincts, she found the strength to act.

Janet took hold of her daughter with both hands. "No!" she said to her husband. "Not like this."

Alex was taken off guard. Before he could take a firm stand against this unwanted intrusion into his handling of the affair, Janet pressed her attack. "The doctor is not to be doubted," she said, using a tone that revealed her trust in him was mostly common courtesy. "And Mary Ellen must be punished. But I will not stand by and let her be scarred by such a weapon."

She yanked the cane out of her husband's hands. "If a grown man's bare hands are not enough to punish a little girl, then the fault lies not with her."

Alex would have grown angry, were he not in such a state of shock. He looked to the doctor with sheepish eyes. The doctor gave him a nod of reassurance. "It's best that the parents are in agreement as to the punishment," he said. "Go ahead and take the girl. I'd like to speak to Mrs. MacDonald."

Alex took a last look at the knotted cane in his wife's hands. Now that the doctor had allowed him to surrender it without a fight, he took the opportunity to pull Mary Ellen from the room without delay.

He led the girl to the back bedroom that the entire family now shared. He made her lie bent over with her upper body on the bed and her feet on the ground. Though her dress would cushion her from the full force of his hand, she had reached an age where it was inappropriate for him to contemplate a bare target. He struck her bottom as it was, covered by her dress and underclothing.

This was better than the cane, or even a switch, but it still hurt. Mary Ellen cried out at each blow.

Alex competed with her cries by making his own noise. "Why must you do such evil things?" he asked. "Why can't you learn the difference between right and wrong?"

Each time he swatted her there came a rhetorical question to buffer the sound of her cries. "How many times must we do this? When will you ever learn?"

After four or five such questions, Mary Ellen noticed that the blows hurt less. Each succeeding spank delivered less force. She worked up the courage to turn her head and look back. Her father's face dripped tears, and he hardly seemed to realize what his arm was doing. "What's wrong with you?" he asked. "Are you sick in the head? Are you truly sick?"

At last, he ceased the feeble blows altogether and buried his face in his hands. "Why can't you be the little girl you used to be?"

Mary Ellen rose and threw her arms around her father. "I'm still that girl. I wish you would believe me."

Alex's hands became tender toward her. He hugged her close. "I wish I could."

Chapter 24

Janet stared past Dr. Prince. She could hear the muffled cries of Mary Ellen from the bedroom as she received her punishment. Both her ears and her eyes trained themselves in that direction.

Dr. Prince shut the kitchen door and interjected himself into her field of vision. "It hurts you, I know. I've worked with countless parents of troubled children. There's always some pain involved in making things right."

"Do you have children of your own?" Janet asked.

"No. I've never been so fortunate."

"Then you don't know. You'll never know."

"Perhaps you're right."

He pulled one of the chairs out from the kitchen table and offered it. "We might be more comfortable seated."

"You go ahead. I don't want to sit." She nodded toward the closed door. "I can't sit while that's going on."

"Very well." He pushed the chair back under the table. "Mrs. MacDonald, I made a mistake. It was stupid, and I apologize for it."

"For what?"

"For not sharing the insights I shared with your husband with you as well. In my defense, I saw that you were feeling poorly, and I didn't want to burden you in your time of illness. But now I see you are as much the foundation of this family as is your husband. I hope you'll forgive me."

"I can easily forgive for that much."

"Good. Thank you. Now then, to correct my error, allow me to catch you up. Having spoken with Mary Ellen at some length, I am convinced she suffers from multiple personalities."

Janet gasped and brought her hand to her mouth.

134

"To put it in common terms, I am now quite sure there is a hidden personality within Mary Ellen that compels her to do these devilish things. The personality of the Mary Ellen you know and love does not know the other exists."

"You've only been here a short time. How can you be sure of such a thing already?"

"I wasn't sure of it, until just a moment ago. It was just a well-founded theory until then."

"What made you sure?"

"Mary Ellen herself made me sure. We all heard it. She said *Mary Ellen* didn't go near the pantry. The normal thing to have said was *I* didn't go near the pantry."

"I didn't notice," Janet lied.

"Hmm." Dr. Prince blinked at her. "I heard her quite plainly. I'm sure your husband did also."

Janet gave no rebuttal. She knew her lie was no deterrent to him.

"When people refer to themselves in the third person, they are either being boorishly pretentious or they are not who they appear to be. Mary Ellen does not have a bit of pretentiousness in her."

Janet finished his syllogism. "Therefore, she's somebody else."

"In that moment she was. Mary Ellen has a latent personality. I'm sure of it now. It makes her do things without the faintest knowledge that she's doing them. That's why she doesn't remember starting the fires."

"Then how can we punish her? It's not her fault." She held her cheeks in her palms and clenched her eyes closed. "We must seem horribly cruel to her."

"Perhaps now, but I'm certain she will give you her thanks one day."

"How could she be thankful for such treatment?"

"As I explained to Mr. MacDonald, the only way to save her is to make the punishments seep down to the underlying personality."

"Punish her more severely for something she hasn't willfully done?"

"In a word, yes. I'm sorry, Mrs. MacDonald, but this is how it must be. I understand it is difficult, but there is no other way."

She pulled the chair back out. "I think I will sit down now."

"Please do. This is difficult news, but the time has come for me to lay it out for you without any sugar coating."

"I don't know if I'll be able to stand it."

"You must, Mrs. MacDonald. For the sake of the child. I thought the devilish personality buried inside Mary Ellen would show itself to us eventually, and it's best for everyone that it did so soon."

As Janet bowed her head and stared at the grain of the wood in the table, Dr. Prince ran his tongue over his teeth in subtle self-congratulation at the fruits of his own cleverness.

Chapter 25

The night nurse came in to check Emma's vitals. Rob and Marcia watched from the other side of Emma's bed. The nurse whispered to them that everything looked stable. When she was done, the nurse asked if they needed anything. "Answers," Rob was tempted to reply, but he knew she had none to give. Besides, something had given him a new confidence regarding Emma's health.

He told the nurse they were fine and waited for her to leave. Then he pulled Marcia into their sleeping corner. "I think she's going to be okay," he whispered.

"She's been the same for hours," Marcia protested. "How can you know that?"

"The same way I know the doctors aren't going to figure out what's wrong with her."

"What? Why not?"

"Because you're right. This thing is way more than a dream. I don't know what it is, but I know it's real, on some level we don't understand. And I also know, he needs her."

"The Gatekeeper?"

"Exactly. He needs her to fulfill whatever mission he's on. He needs us all. This illness isn't a virus or bacteria; it's his doing. He wants her out of touch with us, but he needs her alive. If she dies"—the word stuck in his throat—"everything he's been doing so far is for nothing. He needs his Mary Ellen to do whatever it is he wants her to do, and she can't do that without Emma."

A light went on in Marcia's eyes. "Plus, with her unconscious, he can use her whenever he wants. He doesn't have to wait for her to fall asleep."

"Exactly. He must be closing in on something because he's in a hurry all of a sudden."

The light in Marcia's eyes turned to terror. "What happens when he gets Mary Ellen to do whatever it is he wants? When he doesn't need Emma anymore?"

Rob bit his lip. "Maybe he'll just release his hold on her."

"Do you trust him to do that?"

"Maybe we have to put our trust in ourselves. Maybe there's a way to defeat him before that happens."

"There'd better be, and we'd better find it."

Rob sighed. "If only we had some control over them."

Marcia took his hand. "Maybe we do. I felt like I exerted some influence over Janet this time. When you—when Alex had that cane, I think she would have let him use it if it weren't for me."

"Are you sure?"

Marcia huffed exasperation and shook her head. "No. I'm not sure of anything. It's just a feeling I got, but it's a strong one. I feel like I helped her motherly instincts overcome her old-fashioned obedience to her husband."

"If that's true, we've got to test it and find out how to exploit it. That means we've got to go back, the sooner the better."

Marcia flinched. She hated the idea, but she knew it was right. Still holding Rob's hand, she led him down to the blankets on the floor. "We can do this. We can beat him."

"We have to," he replied.

Chapter 26

Alex picked up the milk pail. It was too early to milk the cows. They'd been fed and there was no tending they needed right now. Maybe it would be okay to milk them a little early. It would give him an excuse to linger in the barn. He wasn't ready to go back into the house with the others.

Mary Ellen would still be in her parents' bed, where he'd left her after her punishment. Janet would be puttering around the house, trying to keep busy so she didn't have to look at anyone or talk about recent events. Alex could avoid them, but Dr. Prince might be lurking anywhere. There was no telling when he might pop up and start lecturing Alex with confusing analyses of his daughter and urging him to beat her at every turn.

Alex shook his head at the milk pail. The cows were likely to get ornery if he got them off their schedule, and there was enough trouble around here as it was. He took up the pitchfork instead. Cows can't have their stalls cleaned often enough. At least he would look busy.

As soon as he picked up the fork, he set it back against the wall. Tilting his head to one side, he walked toward the barn door. That was definitely the sound of a motor car coming up the road. Too many automobiles were showing up here lately. He liked it better when the quiet was rarely disturbed by the sound of their engines. Things were more peaceful back then.

Alex's dolorous eyes followed the black box as it developed into a wheeled vehicle. There were two people in the car, but shaded as they were by the bonnet, he couldn't tell if he knew them. He knew he wasn't expecting any more visitors.

The auto stopped in front of Alex. The passenger was the first to emerge. He was a man of medium build, still in his prime, edging toward middle age. He had a thick, black mustache with matching eyebrows. His hatless head revealed hair thinning into baldness at the top, but with one lonely circular shock of hair making its last stand over his forehead.

The man waited for the driver to emerge before approaching Alex. The driver was an older man, stockier than the first. He looked as though he had lived a hearty life, and despite his age, was not done with it yet. He wore a dark blue, double-breasted uniform, with gold buttons running down the left side of his chest. Like his companion, he had a bushy mustache, except that his was white. On his head he wore some sort of policeman's cap.

The two men approached together. The younger one extended his hand toward Alex. "Are you Mr. MacDonald?"

Alex shook his hand. He didn't know these men and they didn't know him, making him wary of why they had come asking for him. "I'm Alex MacDonald," he replied in the low voice of someone who has second thoughts about answering.

The man looked him in the eyes with the steady forthrightness of someone whose business it is to be confident. Seeing the stranger through Alex's eyes, Rob found something familiar about him. But then there was something familiar about everybody in this weird place. There was always something telltale in the eyes, even when the faces were different. Everybody's eyes were really somebody else's eyes—Janet's and Mary Ellen's he recognized as his own wife's and daughter's, but this man's he couldn't place.

"Glad to meet you, Mr. MacDonald. I'm Harold Whidden of the Halifax Herald."

Alex squinted. "A newspaper man?"

"That's right." He indicated toward the older man beside him. "And this is Detective Carroll of the Provincial Police. He was kind enough to give me a lift out here."

Alex quickly shook hands with the detective. He wasn't sure which was a worse surprise, a newspaper man or the police.

Whidden acted quickly to dispel Alex's confusion. "I was hoping to talk to you, to your whole family really, about this trouble with the fires."

Alex's eyes widened with fear that morphed into embarrassment. "How do you know about the fires, all the way down in Halifax?"

Whidden softened his tone to ease Alex's embarrassment. "Well, you see, Mr. MacDonald, what's going on with your family is quite an unusual phenomenon. It's the kind of thing that makes word spread quickly. And then, of course, when a renowned investigator like Dr. Prince gets involved, people get curious."

Alex looked at the ground and scratched the back of his neck. "I had no idea," he said in a faraway kind of voice.

"No other reporters have been here then?"

Alex shook his head.

Whidden couldn't suppress his smile. "I'm surprised by that, but I can't say I'm not pleased." He straightened his face. "There are readers all over Canada and the United States interested in your story, Mr. MacDonald. I'd be honored if you'd allow me to be the one to relay your experiences to them."

Alex shook his head. "No. I don't think so. This is a private matter. You'd better go and leave us alone."

"With all due respect, Mr. MacDonald, you're wrong about that. Please take this in the friendly vein in which it's intended, but this is no longer a private matter."

Alex tensed and squinted at him. "What do you mean?"

"I mean that what I'm about to tell you may shock and alarm you, but I tell you these things as a friend, because you should know what's going on out there." He waved his arm through the air to indicate the wide world. "At this moment, there are more people than you could guess writing about what's happening here. They don't know you. They don't know your daughter. All they know is

141

what they've heard. They haven't bothered to speak to you, but they've spoken to enough people willing to spread rumors about you. People are speaking for you, and those people are not your friends."

Alex wiped a hand down over his face. He appeared tipsy enough that Whidden put out his arms to support him. Alex pushed his arms away. "I'm all right. I don't need any help." He tried to swallow but his throat was too dry. "What are they saying, these people?"

"I'm afraid it's not flattering," Whidden replied. "The consensus is that your Mary Ellen is a cracked pot. The only thing left up for debate is whether she's crazy enough to actually burn you up in your own house, or you're crazy enough to actually let her."

Alex covered his mouth with his hand. He breathed through his fingers for a while before finding words. "It's all lies. We've got to stop them."

Whidden shook his head. "You can't stop them. But you can tell them the truth. Let me write your story. Together we can correct the lies."

Alex pulled at the hair on the back of his head and kicked at the dirt. "No. I don't know. Everything we do only makes it worse."

From behind him came Janet's voice. "Alex. Who's there? What's going on?"

They all turned to see Mrs. MacDonald coming toward them. She approached with a gait slightly faster than normal for her.

"A newspaper man," Alex told her as she joined them. He said no more, as if that description told her all she needed to know about their dire situation.

Whidden stepped forward and bowed. "Harold Whidden of the Halifax Herald. Mrs. MacDonald, I presume?"

"Yes," she replied.

"He wants to write our story," Alex said.

"Oh, I'm afraid we don't have much of a story, Mr. Whidden. I doubt anyone would be interested in us."

142

"Has Dr. Prince come?" Whidden asked.

"Why yes, but—"

"Mrs. MacDonald, if Dr. Prince is here, there's a story here. If not, he'll make one."

"What do you mean?"

"I was just telling your husband that newsmen, and people of even lower character, all over North America are writing about the happenings on your farm. They are not drawing a proud picture of your daughter. What I have not told your husband yet is that they have all taken their lead from Dr. Prince. Before he ever left Boston, he made his opinions clear regarding your daughter. His primary opinion is the sooner she is locked away in a mental institution, the better."

Janet gasped. "No! He never mentioned anything like that to us!"

Whidden's lips curled into an expression like an unhappy smile. "No. Of course he didn't."

"He came to help us settle things right here." Alex made a wave at the farm. "He never said anything about taking her away."

An odd glow came to Whidden's eyes. "It's true, there are certain things he wants to settle right here. And if he settles them to his satisfaction, the asylum will be the best end Mary Ellen can hope for."

Janet clutched her husband's arm. "Alex, he's scaring me."

Whidden took a half step backward. The glow faded from his eyes. "I'm truly sorry, Mrs. MacDonald. That was not my intent. I only want you to know the gravity of the situation. I can help you if you let me. Please say you'll let me visit with you a while."

"We've already got all the help we can use," Alex answered for them.

Whidden raised his eyebrows toward Janet, asking with them if she shared her husband's opinion.

With some difficulty, she nodded. "I stand with my husband."

"You'll put Mary Ellen's future completely in the hands of Dr. Prince? Even after what he's said about her?"

"He can help us manage her," Alex answered. "All you can do is write stories."

"Stories have more power than you imagine, Mr. MacDonald. They can change people's minds. It would do you a fair bit of good to change some minds about Mary Ellen."

Janet tugged at Alex's arm. "Maybe it would be a good thing to tell our story." She addressed Whidden. "You wouldn't write hurtful things, would you?"

Whidden bowed. "I promise, I would write nothing but the truth."

"I still don't like it," Alex grumbled.

"Alex, I trust this man," Janet said. "He has a fair-minded look to him."

Detective Carroll had been so still and silent as to nearly blend into the background. Now he reminded them of his presence with a short statement. "I've worked with a lot of reporters in my years on the police force. I can assure you Mr. Whidden is the straightest shooter of them all."

"Let him stay, Alex." Janet let herself lean against her husband, allowing him to be her buttress. "Just for a little while."

Alex scrunched up his face and rocked from one foot to the other. Only after he had looked into the pleading eyes of his usually deferential wife, did he speak. "All right. For a while."

A new voice captured the group's attention. It came from behind the MacDonalds. "It's getting awfully crowded around here today," Dr. Prince said.

Janet turned sideways between Whidden and Dr. Prince. "Oh, Dr. Prince, this is Mr. Whidden, from the newspaper. He's going to be visiting with us for a while."

Dr. Prince scowled.

Whidden ignored the scowl. "A pleasure to finally meet you, Doctor. Your reputation looms large, even in our little province." He nodded to his companion. "This is Detective Carroll."

Dr. Prince made no effort to shake hands. His scowl coalesced around his mouth. "I appreciate your interest in this case, gentlemen, but this family must have privacy in order for us to make meaningful progress."

"I promise you. We will be completely unintrusive," Whidden said.

Dr. Prince's eyes flashed. "You are intrusive merely by standing where you stand."

Whidden flashed a mischievous smile. "I'm sorry you feel that way, Doctor. Would you like us to stand over there?" He pointed to a patch of ground several feet away.

"I'd prefer you stand in Halifax, if you must know." He turned toward the MacDonalds. "There are altogether too many people here for us to do any meaningful work. Someone has to go."

"I'm sorry, Dr. Prince," Janet replied, "but we've already invited these men to stay."

Whidden stepped forward. "Excuse me, Mrs. MacDonald, but the doctor makes a good point. Maybe someone should go away from here. May I suggest yourself and your daughter?"

Janet and Alex joined Dr. Prince in showing alarmed curiosity to him.

"It would be a helpful experiment, don't you think?" Whidden eyed Dr. Prince. "If your theory is that Mary Ellen is behind the fires, why not remove her from the home? See if anything happens in her absence."

Janet searched her husband's face. "That makes sense, don't you think, Alex?"

"It's a waste of time." Dr. Prince waved off the notion with his hands. "Who else could be starting the fires? The question isn't who is starting the fires; it's how to get her to stop."

145

"Maybe to you, Doctor," Whidden replied. "But I'm still not sure who's starting the fires." He looked sympathetically into Janet's eyes. "And I'm not sure Mrs. MacDonald is either."

"This is ridiculous!" Dr. Prince huffed. "There is no one else who could possibly have set the fires."

"Perhaps there is no one"—Whidden looked around the air over their heads—"but is there no *thing*?"

Dr. Prince expelled a snort. "Are you suggesting ghosts are responsible? If so, I'd better have a talk with your editor."

"I suggest nothing except that some honest investigation be done before conclusions are drawn—conclusions that could ruin the life of a little girl."

The doctor threw up his arms. "Wonderful! Let's spend our time hunting ghosts."

"Or maybe just the truth," Whidden replied.

"Where would we go?" Janet asked without waiting for more from Dr. Prince.

"Do you have a neighbor who would take you in for the night?" Whidden asked.

Janet turned to her husband. "You think the McGillivrays would have us?"

"I guess so. They're good folks and we've done them a good turn or two."

"Would you mind driving them, Detective?" Whidden asked his companion.

Detective Carroll shook his head. "Not at all."

Janet began toward the house. "I'll pack some things."

Before she had taken two steps, Dr. Prince placed himself at her side. "My time here is limited. Take her away and you are seriously curtailing the time I can spend with her."

"She needs a good night's rest. We'll come back tomorrow. Early as you please." She stepped past him and went to the house.

Dr. Prince turned to Alex. His eyes accused the family of making a serious mistake. Alex shrugged and looked away. Dr. Prince turned and stormed off toward the house.

Whidden blew air through his teeth as he watched Dr. Prince go away. "He certainly is an opinionated fellow," he said to no one. "I daresay, he sees us as regular flies in his ointment." Addressing Alex, he asked, "How'd he find his way to you?"

Alex hemmed in embarrassment before formulating his reply. "I'm really not sure. I don't know why he chose to come here."

"He just showed up?"

Alex waved off that notion vehemently, reclaiming his control over his home. "Oh no. We got a letter from him a few weeks ago. He said how he heard about Mary Ellen and would like to visit her. Said he was the most successful doctor at handling these sorts of things, and he wouldn't take any payment for coming. The letter said if we didn't write back to him and tell him we didn't want him, he would take that to mean he was to come ahead."

"I take it you didn't tell him not to come."

Alex slid back toward embarrassment. "Well, I meant to tell him just that, but I ain't much of a letter writer. I didn't know quite what to say, and by the time I got around to it, well, there was another little fire. Janet said maybe if Dr. Prince was an expert on such things, and since he was willing to come all the way out here for free, maybe it wouldn't be so bad to just let him come along anyway."

Whidden nodded. "And here he is. But what I'd really like to know is how did he hear about Mary Ellen in the first place?"

Alex was the picture of befuddlement. "I didn't think anybody knew about her at all until we heard from him. We don't make a show of our family business. And now you say the whole world is reading about us."

"Dr. Prince doesn't go anywhere or do anything quietly, if he can help it," Whidden said. "He'll make a public show of any family's business, if it keeps his name in the paper."

"You don't think he's fake, do you? We thought about that for a while, but then what use would it be to anybody to come all the way out here to fake such a thing? I could see if he was asking for money, but he ain't, and we don't have much anyway. It don't make no sense for him to try to hoodwink us over such a thing."

"No, it doesn't. And I don't think he has any interest in whatever money you have. I believe he's here strictly on account of Mary Ellen, and he couldn't be more serious in his purpose."

Alex nodded at the reassuring words. It was a short nod, ended by his eroding confidence that the words were indeed reassuring. They echoed in his head, more ominous than comforting.

Chapter 27

As soon as the physician left the room, Marcia slumped into the hospital chair beside Emma's bed. "I don't know if I can endure another day of this," she told her husband.

"At least they feel confident she's in no immediate danger."

Marcia huffed and expressed a pained grimace. "Why are we even talking about it? They're never going to find out what's wrong with her."

"Not without knowing about this Nova Scotia business, and they won't believe a word of it if we try to tell them."

"We've got to figure out what this game is all about."

"The thing I can't figure out is, why not knock us out, too? Why just Emma? Then he could use us all whenever he wanted."

"Emma's been there longer. She knows more about it. Emma knows something he doesn't want her to tell us."

"What could she know?"

Marcia got up from her chair. She paused to kiss her daughter on the cheek before taking her husband by the hand and leading him to the corner where their blankets were spread. "*We're* still able to talk, so let's talk it out and see if we can get anywhere with it."

They sat against the wall, talking quietly while watching Emma. "What about this Whidden character?" Marcia asked.

"He seems really familiar, but I don't know where I've seen him before. He's got the same thing with the eyes as Janet and Mary Ellen. I recognize Janet's and Mary Ellen's eyes because I'd know you two anywhere. But his eyes I can't place. He's somebody I've seen before, but not often."

"I had the same feeling. I've seen him before too. It's not that I recognize his face, but there's something familiar in the eyes. It's the same as with Alex and Mary Ellen. They don't look like you and Emma so much that I'd call it close to a perfect match, but I can see you two in their eyes."

"What about the others? Dr. Prince and this Detective Carroll."

"Not so much. Dr. Prince has something vaguely familiar in the way he carries himself, but there's nothing I recognize in his eyes. And there's nothing familiar about Carroll. What do you think?"

"No. Neither is familiar to me at all."

Marcia pursed her lips and searched the space around her with her eyes. "So, Whidden is familiar to us both. Dr. Prince is possibly familiar to me only. Carroll is a complete unknown. Can we put anything together from that?"

Rob shrugged. "Should any of this make sense?"

"Yes," Marcia answered quickly. "It all sort of does. Only we don't have enough information to put it together. Back to Whidden. He says he wants to help Mary Ellen, but does he really?"

"Dr. Prince says he's there to help Mary Ellen, but I haven't seen him do anything helpful yet. Same could be true of Whidden."

"Maybe, but he seems more straightforward than Dr. Prince. I like his eyes better."

"Me too. But then why does he want to separate us? I think it'd be better if we stuck together."

"He's not trying to separate us. He's trying to get Mary Ellen away from Dr. Prince. At least, that's what I think. That's why I helped him get Alex to agree to it."

"You helped him? You mean Janet helped him."

"No. I mean I did. I feel like I'm exerting more of my will over her. I don't think she would have stepped in like that on her own. I'm working hard on her, because we need her to do the right thing."

"I don't exert any influence over Alex," Rob admitted.

"Because Alex is too confused. He's torn between his loyalty to his daughter and his need to be logical. He'll do what Dr. Prince tells him because he's bound by his old-fashioned respect for the man's title. Janet, on the other hand, is focused on Mary Ellen. She doesn't necessarily love her more than Alex does; she loves her differently, like a mother does. She'll break down every barrier and defy logic to save her daughter. I think that's why I can get through to her."

Rob yawned. "Sorry. I'm just suddenly so sleepy. I don't know why."

Marcia pulled his head down onto her lap. "Take a nap. I'll watch Emma."

"No. I want to stay here with you. I can sleep later."

She held his head down. "Rob, someone's calling you. You'd better go. It's okay if you can't control anything. Just take in as much as you can, so we can try to figure it out when you get back."

She needn't have tried to convince him. The call was too strong. He was already asleep.

Chapter 28

Someone was shaking him. "MacDonald, are you awake?"

It was dark and the surface he slept on was hard. This wasn't his bed. "Where am I?" he thought. The hand rocking him awake shook memory into him. He was on the floor of his bedroom. Mr. Whidden and Detective Carroll shared the bed. Dr. Prince slept alone in Mary Ellen's room.

Whidden had made notes about the barn and house while Carroll drove Janet and Mary Ellen to the McGillivrays. Dr. Prince hadn't emerged from Mary Ellen's room all evening. By the time Carroll returned, it was late. Alex invited the two newcomers to take his bed for the night, insisting that he would sleep on the floor.

"MacDonald, are you awake?"

He shook off his grogginess. "Uh. What is it?"

"It may seem an odd question, but did you strike me just now?" By the dim moonlight penetrating the window, he could see it was Whidden who addressed him. The reporter leaned over him from the bed. Detective Carroll sat up on the far side of the bed.

"What? No. Why?"

"You were asleep until I shook you?" Whidden asked.

"Yes."

"I thought so, but I wanted to hear it from you just the same."

"Why? What's the matter?" Alex asked.

"It's the strangest thing. You see, I was lying here, wide awake when I began hearing strange noises from the upstairs. I thought it was merely Dr. Prince shuffling around, but it went on for some time. Since I couldn't imagine what would cause him to move about so much, I began to have my doubts that it was him at all. That's right about the time I felt it."

"Felt what?" asked Alex.

"Well, it was a rather sharp blow on my arm. The left one, right above the elbow. I thought Detective Carroll had rolled into me, but he was quite on the opposite edge of the bed. I asked him if he'd struck me on the arm." Whidden turned toward the policeman. "And what did you reply, Carroll?"

"I said of course I hadn't, but that I'd felt an odd pressure applied to the same spot on my left arm."

Whidden turned back to Alex. "It's quite unlikely you could have struck me there without my sensing your approach, Mr. MacDonald, but being a reporter, I wished to assume nothing. This is why I woke you."

Alex was all confusion. Nothing Whidden said made any sense. "I didn't hear any noises or touch anyone," Alex said.

"I know you didn't. And I know Detective Carroll didn't, either. It was someone, or rather, something else. Can you feel it?"

Alex gazed around the dark room for something sensible to latch onto. "Feel what?"

"Its presence. There's something in this house—something alive but not human. Can you feel it all around us?"

Alex shook his head in the dark. "I don't know what you mean."

Whidden turned to Detective Carroll. "What about you, Carroll? Can you feel it?"

"After what I just felt on my arm, I'm not sure I trust my senses anymore. I have a queer feeling, but I can't tell you why."

"It's fading," Whidden said. "It's leaving. Whatever it is, it's going away from here. Fading. Fading. There, it's gone."

Alex sat on the floor in silence. He could make sense of nothing that had just happened.

Detective Carroll spoke. "What do you make of it, Whidden?"

"It's the most peculiar thing I've ever experienced. I have no idea what it all means, except that maybe there is another possible source for the trouble here that no one's yet considered."

153

"You mean some sort of spirit?" Carroll asked.

"I guess that's as good a word as any. How do you feel about that notion, Mr. MacDonald? What if it were some sort of spirit lighting those fires, and not Mary Ellen?"

"I never put much stock in spirits or nothing like that," Alex replied. Then, after a moment's reflection, he added. "But I guess I could start if it got me the old Mary Ellen back."

"That's right, Mr. MacDonald. I find it's best to keep an open mind about these things."

"If there was a spirit," Alex asked, "how would we discover it?"

"A good question, Mr. MacDonald. Maybe Dr. Prince can help us answer that. But for now, whatever might have been here seems to be gone, so I suggest we get some sleep." He lay himself back down. Detective Carroll followed his lead.

Alex lay back on the floor, but he could not return to sleep. He wrestled with this idea of a spirit doing mischief at his home. The idea did not fit very well in his level head. He'd never seen a ghost, and he put little faith in those who claimed they had. Ghosts were for children, the unhinged, and the lazy-minded.

Yet, what Whidden and Carroll had experienced was not easily explained. If they had been men less respectable than a newspaper reporter and a police officer, he might have shrugged off their recital as utter nonsense. But, he assumed, men like these had seen much of the world and were not prone to histrionics over an unexplained bump in the night.

Then there was Mary Ellen to think of. If ghosts made no sense, neither did the apparent change in Mary Ellen. She was a good girl. She'd always been good. She had made him love her as much as he could have loved his own natural child. The notion that she should suddenly begin starting fires that could eventually kill them all was as incredible as the idea of blaming it all on ghosts. The evidence damned her, sure enough, but only when one ruled out the equally unreasonable possibility of evil spirits.

Alex juggled these possibilities through the remains of the night. His reverie was undisturbed by further incidents. He felt no queer sensations nor heard any strange noises. All that came to his ears was the sounds of the two men snoring in the bed, ending when they awoke shortly after dawn.

Alex took them to the kitchen and fed them some pork and lopsided biscuits. It wasn't anything like Janet could have fixed, but the men were appreciative and counted it a hearty breakfast. Dr. Prince came down and joined them. A good night's rest seemed to have done his disposition some good, and he hardly gritted his teeth at all when he spoke.

Alex related to Dr. Prince the strange phenomena Mr. Whidden had experienced during the night. Dr. Prince's natural reaction was to frown skepticism at the men as the story unfolded. Perhaps noting how deeply affected Alex seemed to be, he modified his frown into a wistful smile. He let Alex finish the telling without making any comment or uttering one of the dismissive sounds that periodically yearned to escape him.

When Alex was done speaking, Dr. Prince agreed it was all a very interesting adventure but asserted there was certainly an innocent explanation for the men's experiences.

Whidden spoke. "You have some experience in investigating the supernatural, don't you, Doctor?"

"Yes," Dr. Prince replied. "I've investigated numerous so-called clairvoyants, making claims to be in communication with the spirits of those passed, and I've proved them to be frauds."

"All of them?" Whidden asked.

"Yes. For the most part." Dr. Prince coughed lightly. "There was only one very clever lady I could not catch at her game. She was a fraud like all the others, but I couldn't find enough evidence to prove it."

"Then how do you know?" Whidden asked.

"Because they are all frauds. There is no communication between living people and spirits."

"But you couldn't prove it, in all cases."

"I could smell it!" The doctor's nostrils flared. "The impossible can only seem possible through fraud."

"I wonder, Doctor," Whidden mused, "if you would be willing to attempt a little experiment regarding spirits."

"Do you now claim to be in touch with the dead? An odd position for a newspaper reporter."

"Well, I have been sensing a strange presence off and on since the incident Mr. MacDonald told you about. I feel as if there is someone or something hovering near about. I feel as if this presence is trying to communicate with me. I wonder, with your knowledge of the practices of clairvoyants, if you'd be willing to try to make contact."

"Nonsense!" Dr. Prince erupted in indignant huffs. "I told you that was all rubbish."

"Then what's the harm in it? If it fails, as you seem certain it will, it will give you evidence to support your position."

"I need no more evidence."

"Come now, Doctor. What's the harm?" Whidden pressed. "Mr. MacDonald, wouldn't you like to know one way or the other if there is some entity that could shed light on your troubles and bring relief to your family?"

Alex was taken aback that this discussion had come around to involving him. He recoiled from the pairs of eyes now staring at him.

From within, Rob wished Alex to take whatever steps might renew Alex's faith in his daughter. Rob strained to send his energy to convince Alex to reach for any straw that might save Mary Ellen.

Alex planted himself and mumbled, "I suppose it wouldn't hurt to try whatever we can."

"See there, Doctor?" Whidden said. "You can hardly turn your back on poor MacDonald."

Cornered, Dr. Prince scowled.

"I'm particularly interested in the methods of the one lady you call clever. Do you recall how she raised the spirits?"

"Yes. I recall her act quite well," Dr. Prince grumbled.

"Could you recreate it for us now? I'm beginning to feel the presence getting stronger."

The doctor sighed. "Very well. Whatever will give you a story so you can go and leave me to the real work to be done."

"Excellent! You're a fine fellow, Dr. Prince." Whidden searched around them. "I suppose this table will do, but we should have paper. If something communicates to us, we'll want to write it down. I have some news-copy paper in my bag. Would you be so kind as to retrieve it from the bedroom for me, Mr. MacDonald?"

When Alex returned with the bag, Whidden took a stack of paper from within and placed it on the table before him. Alex took his seat to the right of Whidden at the square table. Detective Carroll sat across from the newsman while Dr. Prince occupied the seat to his left.

Whidden extracted several Ever-Sharp pencils from his bag and laid them down next to the paper. "Now then, Dr. Prince," he began. "are we to all join hands? That seems to be the common practice in these situations."

Dr. Prince rolled his eyes. "As you wish." The men around the table joined hands.

"From here, I bow to your expertise, Doctor." Whidden tilted his head toward Dr. Prince. "Although I suspect the techniques of the woman who was never proven a fraud might be most productive of our time."

"Quiet! Bow your heads and close your eyes, and let us get this childish display done with."

The doctor intoned the words he had learned in his investigations to summon spirits to the world of the living, though he spoke them with less than full enthusiasm. Alex peeked through his eyelids at

157

the unlikely scene around him. He was uncomfortable and expected nothing from the demonstration, but the world had already quit making sense, so he sat quietly and waited.

At last, Dr. Prince finished his recitation and fell to silence. Whidden, head bowed and eyes closed, asked out the side of his mouth. "Is that it?"

"That's it. You can see how productive it was."

Whidden opened his left eye and peered at the doctor through it. "You might have put a little more spirit into it."

"That's the trouble. There is no spirit in it. It's all sham." Dr. Prince let go of the hands of the men on either side of him, smirking his failure as a clairvoyant at them. The others let go of each other's hands. "Now, can you finish up with whatever you came here to do so I can get on with my work?"

Whidden opened his mouth to speak, but no words came. Instead, his mouth issued a sound like a sustained dog's whining. His pupils dilated and he stared at the table before him as in a catatonic trance.

"Whidden, what is it?" Carroll asked. He flashed his hand in front of the newsman's face. Whidden's eyes stared through it.

After half a minute, Whidden's whining tailed off into silence. Without moving his eyes, he took up a pencil and moved the paper into the focal spot of his vision. His hand moved violently across the paper, his knuckles white with stress from squeezing the pencil. The others craned to see what he was writing but the fury with which his hand moved prevented them from making out the words. Even the hand with which he held the paper shook, making it impossible for any of them to focus upon the words at the top as his pencil hand moved down the page.

"What is this? A joke?" Dr. Prince puffed. But even he was impressed by the speed at which the newsman wrote. Though he might wish it to be a mere prank, his eyes wondered at the sincerity of Whidden's actions.

Whidden threw the first sheet to the side and moved his pencil to the top of the second. This page he filled with the same vigor as the first. Dr. Prince slid the first sheet toward himself and began reading. The hurried penmanship of the writer was not easy to decipher, and as the other two men looked on, Whidden finished filling the second sheet before Dr. Prince had read half the first.

Whidden threw the second sheet to the side and began the third. Neither Carroll nor Alex touched the second sheet, but rather waited for Dr. Prince to move on to it. By the time he did this, Whidden was through his third sheet. After the fourth sheet was tossed to the side, Carroll took up sheets three and four, but only long enough to arrange them in the proper order for Dr. Prince. This he did after each new sheet was cast aside.

When Dr. Prince was safely buried in his backlog of reading, Whidden changed his pattern. Instead of tossing each finished sheet onto the pile, he kept odd ones to himself and piled them on his lap. This he did only when Dr. Prince was thoroughly engrossed in his reading. Carroll and Alex watched this change without comment, not wishing to impose themselves onto this surreal situation.

After the sixth or seventh sheet, Whidden exhausted the lead in his pencil. The metallic tip tore into the paper rather than writing on it. Realizing the tear in the paper, Whidden cast the pencil aside so that it rolled off the table. Carroll pushed one of his reserve pencils toward him. Whidden picked it up without turning his head from his work. He continued his furious writing as if nothing had interrupted it.

Whidden wrote and Dr. Prince read for what seemed a long time to Alex. In all that time, Whidden did not look up from his writing. He merely cast filled sheets of paper off to the side or piled them on his lap, as the whim of whatever spirit controlled him dictated. Dr. Prince looked up from his reading only a handful of times, when overcome by the urge to share a frown with the onlookers or sigh his skepticism at them. Carroll worked his role as organizer of the sheets Whidden cast upon the table, keeping them in the proper order for Dr. Prince's reading. Whenever Whidden cast an empty metal shell of a pencil aside, Carroll pushed another toward him.

Alex moved only his eyes. His body remained motionless, sending its energy to his spinning mind. His thoughts struggled, wondering how his life had come to this moment and where it could possibly go from here. He was a simple man, mismatched with troubles that were far too complex for him. These sorts of difficulties were meant for men who had minds for puzzles. It wasn't right that they were laid at the doorstep of a man who wanted nothing more than to be left alone in his world of basic routine.

After a long time, Whidden threw a final sheet of paper into the pile on the table and slapped his pencil down. He shook his head as if freeing his mind from the cobwebs of a heavy blow to his skull. He rubbed the back of his neck. "What happened?"

The others eyed him in disbelief. Alex's and Carroll's disbeliefs were rooted in amazement; Dr. Prince's was of the cynical brand. "You've been writing for nearly an hour," Carroll told Whidden.

"An hour?" Whidden replied. "Why, MacDonald just brought me the paper a minute ago."

Carroll now demonstrated some of his policeman's logic. "At what time did Mr. MacDonald bring you the paper?"

"I checked my watch while I waited for him. It was almost nine, making it probably just nine now."

Carroll pulled his own watch from his pocket, popped it open, and showed it to Whidden. The hour hand pointed to ten. The minute hand approached twelve. Whidden considered. "In that case, I'd like to know"—he rubbed the back of his head—"which one of you gentlemen ambushed me with the skillet. My ears are still ringing from the blow."

Alex put up his hands to ward off the accusation. "Not a one of us came near you."

Carroll added, "You fell into some kind of trance."

"Without nobody doing a thing to you," Alex said.

"And I wrote something?" Whidden asked.

Carroll tilted his head toward Dr. Prince. "The doctor's got it."

All eyes turned toward Dr. Prince, who was still flipping through the sheets of paper in his hands.

"Well-crafted work, I hope," Whidden said of the writing. "I have a reputation to uphold."

Dr. Prince looked up at him over the papers. "Though I'm sure you are a fine wordsmith, well-crafted work would not fit your game in this instance. These scribbles are pure stream of consciousness, as is to be expected. No one would count on careful prose from a tortured soul of the spirit world, eh?"

"What's it say?" Carroll asked.

"Well, it appears as though our mystery is solved. For here is the confession of the guilty party. It seems the spirit who possessed our friend"—Dr. Prince pointed with the papers toward Whidden— "performed all the mischief and started all the fires in this home. It's all right here on paper. That's the first part of it anyway. The rest is some sort of impromptu treatise on the existence of a spirit world and the interactions of the residents therein with our own world. Indeed, a lot of ground is covered in this volume."

"And you say I wrote all that?" Whidden looked around the table to share the question with all of them.

"You certainly did," Dr. Prince answered. "Only, I suggest next time you want to play such a longwinded joke, you bring along a typewriter. It would make it easier on both your hand and my eyes."

"You think this is a joke?" Whidden asked.

"Of course it is, and I have no more time for jokes." Dr. Prince threw the papers on the table and marched out of the kitchen.

Carroll took the papers and rifled through them, his investigative curiosity getting the better of him.

Whidden stood up. "Mr. MacDonald, do you think you could help me find a cool cloth for my head?"

161

Alex got him a cloth and took him to the pump. As Alex pumped water onto the cloth, Whidden took the papers he had held on his lap, folded them, and stuffed them into Alex's pocket. "Read these, when you find them again."

Chapter 29

When Rob rustled awake, he was alone in the corner of the room. Marcia stood beside Emma's bed, holding the little girl's hand. Evening shadows had begun stretching across the room.

The sight of Marcia holding Emma's hand sent a wave of panic through Rob. He scrambled to his feet and hurried to Marcia's side. "What's the matter?" he asked. "Did something happen?"

"Nothing," Marcia answered in a hollow voice. "Doctors and nurses came through. "They all had something to say, but none of it mattered. They don't know anything we didn't know yesterday."

"Why didn't you wake me?"

"I couldn't chance it. We were learning nothing new here, but you might be learning something that could help us where you were. I didn't want to bring you back too soon." She let her eyes fall. "And besides, if you were in the middle of something over there, I wasn't sure I'd be able to wake you, and that scared me."

She'd made the right choice. He nodded approval.

She turned toward him. "How are you feeling?"

He motioned toward Emma. "If she's okay, I'm okay."

"You were out a long time."

"Looks like most of the afternoon," he replied.

"What happened? Tell me everything. We've got to start figuring this out." She rubbed a forming tear from her eye.

The tear finished her thought. They had to figure it out before it was too late to help Emma.

Rob told her everything he'd seen through Alex's eyes. From the odd occurrences in the night bedroom to Whidden's apparent spirit possession.

163

As Rob recounted watching Whidden scribble his possessed writings, Marcia interrupted him. "I want to hear the rest, but I have to tell you something else. That all really happened. When you were sleeping, I looked up more stuff on my phone. Whidden was a real guy. He and Carroll were really there, just like Dr. Prince."

"And you're telling me the real Whidden was possessed by a spirit, too?"

"Exactly. At least he thought he was. He wrote an account of his experiences with the MacDonalds. It sounds just like what you've been telling me. He was so messed up by it that he couldn't even bring himself to write down everything that happened. He just wrote the stuff he thought people could handle, and even that, he wouldn't publish. It only turned up after he died."

"Was there anything in it that might help us?"

She shook her head a little. "It's so hard to tell. I'm not even sure if I read the complete account or just a snippet. The only impression I could get is that he had a lot of sympathy for the MacDonalds, especially Mary Ellen. He seemed like a good guy. A lot better vibe than Dr. Prince."

"Well, since you've been reading ahead, is there anybody else I should be on the lookout for when I go to sleep again?"

Marcia thought for a moment, then shook her head. "No. I can't remember coming across anybody else who played a meaningful role."

"Okay, I probably should have asked this before, but how does this all end? I mean, in the real story, how did it end?"

"That's the frustrating part. I couldn't find out anything much about that. It's almost like the world lost interest in the whole thing and it just faded away. I read that the MacDonalds moved away from the farm, but I couldn't tell if they came back. And there are hints Mary Ellen was institutionalized for a while, but I couldn't find anything that said that for sure."

"Too bad we don't have a plumber handy to ask these things."

164

"Yeah, you've got that right. But I'm not sure it really matters how it ended. I mean, is there any guarantee it will end the same way this time?"

"Who knows?" Rob squinted and raised a finger. "Wait. Back up a minute. When you read about Whidden being possessed by spirits, was he writing things down at the time?"

"Yes. He wrote quite a lot that day, actually."

"What happened to everything he wrote?"

"You mean the actual papers? I guess he must have kept it all. That's probably what he used to write his account later on."

"Was there any mention of him giving any of the papers to Alex?"

"I don't remember any."

"So, he didn't push any of them into Alex's pocket?"

"I don't know." Marcia instinctively glanced at the front pockets of the pants Rob had worn for the past three days. She pointed to the pocket on the left side. "What's that?"

Rob saw it and felt it at the same time. Protruding from his pocket was the edge of a mass of folded papers.

He pulled the mass from his pocket and unfolded it. It was at least a dozen pages thick, the top page covered with hurried cursive, written in pencil. He squinted at the familiar parcel, mumbling to himself, "It's impossible. It can't be."

"It can't be what?"

His eyes grew wide and his face white.

"Rob? What's going on?"

"It's Whidden's paper. How can that be?"

Marcia guided him to a chair. "It can be. Because it's always been real. Our dream world has been a real world all along. It's just a different world. Emma was right from the beginning: it's no dream; it's the other place."

"But how could this paper come back with me?"

165

Marcia turned on a lamp beside the chair. "It doesn't matter. Just read it to me."

As Marcia stood and stroked her daughter's hand, Rob sat under the light and softly read.

Dear Robert and Marcia,

I cannot explain everything that is happening to you. Time is short and I must fit much into these lines. Dr. Prince is right; the trance I am writing this under is a hoax, not because there are no spirits in this house, but because there are: Dr. Prince and myself. Just as your family has become the MacDonalds in this existence, so have we taken the places of Dr. Prince and Whidden. We control our characters while you are unwilling observers.

Whidden and Dr. Prince are real people, but in this instance, they have been possessed (for lack of a better word) by myself and another spirit. If you have not guessed it, the other spirit is the one you call the Gatekeeper. Who I am is not important. I stand in direct opposition to him and all he attempts.

We are both servants of powerful masters. A century ago, the Gatekeeper's master sent him to work evil among the MacDonald family. He caused Mary Ellen to do all manner of mischief. His ultimate assignment was to coax young Mary Ellen into murdering her parents. Mary Ellen's resolve proved too weak for this, and the Gatekeeper failed his master.

His master was displeased and caused the Gatekeeper to roam the Earth, searching for the perfect family to play the roles of the MacDonalds so he could have another go at it. He needed a firm-

166

willed child who might also be persuaded to do things running against her nature. The souls of the family needed to match quite perfectly. It took him many years to find the family he sought, but he finally found success in you.

I use the term souls for lack of a better word. It is merely a term you are familiar with in place of a truth you are not. The concept is beyond your current understanding. In many ways, you are nothing like the MacDonalds. The only outward sign of your match is in the eyes.

Don't worry over Emma's current condition. She is not harmed. The Gatekeeper is keeping her from consciousness in order to prevent her from divulging what I have just told you—he has taken the form of Dr. Prince. He will not harm her as long as she is the key to carrying out his plans.

He did not want you to know his true identity because the longer you inhabit the MacDonalds the more influence you will learn to wield over them. If you know not to trust Dr. Prince, distrust of him will grow within the MacDonalds. You can turn the MacDonalds against him. It may make him more desperate and dangerous, but you are better off armed with this knowledge.

The Gatekeeper does not know who I am, but he must by now suspect I'm not the real Whidden, which tells him my nature. He will try to pull you away from me. He will soon surmise I have revealed his secret to you. The good: he will have no more reason to keep Emma in her current condition. She is harder to manipulate in this unnatural unconsciousness in which she now lies. The bad: he will become more desperate than ever.

Exert as much influence as you can over the MacDonalds. Every bit helps, but the majority weight of it all will still come down on Emma. She must display courage beyond her years if you are to be saved. This is no dream—it is a very real world. Any harm, even fatality, befalling any of the MacDonalds will befall the one of you who inhabits that MacDonald.

Emma is the key. She must remain strong. She will be called upon to do the most difficult thing. It will be the hardest thing she will ever do. It may not seem right, but it will be the only choice that can save her family. She will recognize this path. In a split second she must choose it. When she wakes, you must train this notion into her. She must do the hardest thing of all, and she must do it swiftly. If she does, I can save you. You must have faith in me. It is the only way. I can only save you if she does that which will seem most terrible to her.

I can't write more. Dr. Prince grows tired of my séance. I must stop.

Your friend.

Rob looked up from the papers.

"'Your friend' who?" Marcia asked.

Rob held up the last page for her. "I don't know. That's all it says."

She took the entire stack from him and read them over to herself. He waited until he could see she had finished. "So?" he asked.

"We were right not to trust Prince. The Gatekeeper shielded his eyes from me, but I must have noted his mannerisms without even realizing it. Whoever our friend is, he's right. Remember I told you Prince carried himself in a familiar way. He carries himself just like the Gatekeeper does."

"That's why I didn't recognize him," Rob said. "I never saw the Gatekeeper."

"So, is he supposed to be Satan or something?"

Rob laughed a pitiful chuckle. "Satan? I have to admit I never put much stock in Satan. And none of this changes my mind. I don't feel like Satan has to go back and try again? I think when Satan loses, he moves on to the next thing. This isn't Satan. This is an evil far more persistent."

Marcia shook her head. "Those poor people!"

"We'd better start thinking about *poor us*," Rob countered. "We've got to get out of this."

Marcia shook her head. "No. We've got to get Prince, or the Gatekeeper, or whoever the hell he is, out of this. If that letter was right, which there's no reason to doubt, there are only two ways this can end. Either he wins and Mary Ellen kills her parents, or we find a way to beat him, and he has to wait around for another hundred years or whatever it takes to find somebody else."

"And if Mary Ellen kills her parents . . ." Rob stopped mid-thought and stared at his wife.

"Emma kills us," Marcia finished for him.

Rob shook off the idea in short, rigorous movements of his head. "She would never. She couldn't do it."

"No," Marcia agreed. "Not in our world. But in that other place, who knows what unnatural influence Prince holds over her. If he really is some sort of evil spirit, we can't begin to guess what he can make anyone do."

Rob knotted his fingers into his hair. "This can't be happening. How can this be happening? It all defies logic."

"Maybe it's not logical. Maybe it makes no sense at all. But it is real. We're living it, and we've got to attack it like it's the most real thing on Earth."

Rob slapped his hands down on the arms of the chair. He breathed a long breath, thrusting himself up from the chair. "Okay, then let's beat the son of a bitch at his own game."

He pulled Marcia to him and held her tight.

"Let's do what we've got to do," he said. "We'll make Alex and Janet do the right things. We'll dig as deep as we have to and bend them to our wills."

Marcia let her head fall onto his shoulder. It made her feel better knowing her husband was no longer limited by logic. Now that he had broken free of denial, they were that much stronger. "Emma has the most control of any of us. Remember what the letter said? We've got to prepare her to do whatever needs to be done."

"Then that's just what we'll do." Rob's voice was firm with determination. "She's a strong child with strong parents. I have faith in her. Emma will do the right thing."

Emma sat up in the bed.

Chapter 30

Emma's parents were instantly at her bedside. Marcia laid her hands on Emma's arm. "Oh Em! Are you okay?"

At the same time, Rob asked. "How do you feel?"

Emma squeezed her eyes shut for a second. She leaned toward her mother and Marcia took her into her arms. "Mommy, I was so scared!"

"It's all right now, sweetie. Mommy and Daddy are right here with you. You don't have to be scared."

"I know. I could hear you sometimes when you were talking to the doctors. I wanted to talk to you, but I couldn't. It was so scary."

Rob stroked his daughter's hair. "It's okay now. You can talk to us."

"Yeah, but how do I know he won't do it to me again?"

Marcia took a step back and looked into Emma's eyes. "The Gatekeeper?"

"Yeah. He wouldn't let me wake up because he didn't want me to tell you he's also Dr. Prince."

"We know he is, sweetie. He's a bad man, but he has no reason not to let you wake up now that we know his secret. We know it and we're going to beat him."

Tears trickled down Emma's cheeks. "I wish I knew how to beat him. But he can do magic stuff, and we can't." She let out a large sob. "He wants me to shoot Mary Ellen's parents with a gun."

Marcia's eyes met Rob's as she spoke to her daughter. "He wants Mary Ellen to do it, not you."

Emma shook her head. "He can't get Mary Ellen to do it. He said she's too weak. So now he wants me to do it for her. I'm scared of guns, but maybe if it will get him to leave us all alone—"

"No!" Marcia lifted Emma's head and locked eyes with her. "You can't do it. If you shoot her parents . . ." Instead of finishing her thought, she bit her lip.

"If you shoot her parents"—Rob stepped in—"you'll be doing something very bad because it's the easy way out. Sometimes doing the right thing is hard. Sometimes it's the hardest thing you've ever had to do, but it's still the right thing."

Emma nodded at him. "I'm glad you said so. I don't want to shoot anybody."

"Emma, listen," Rob went on. "While you were sleeping here in the hospital, I found a friend in the other place. He's got some magic powers, just like the Gatekeeper, only he does good things with them. He's going to help us."

"Who is he? Is he coming to the farm?"

Rob tried to think back. "I don't know how much you saw of him, but he was the man who came to the farm and sent Mary Ellen and her mom to the neighbors."

Emma considered this. "I remember Mary Ellen's mom coming to get her in the house and then bringing her out to that old-fashioned car. There was a policeman driving the car. There was a man talking with Mary Ellen's dad and he winked at her when she went to the car. That's all I remember. Then I woke up here."

"The man talking to Mary Ellen's dad," Rob said. "He's the one who will help us."

"He has magic powers too? Just like the Gatekeeper?"

"Yes. Just like the Gatekeeper."

"Is he going to beat up the Gatekeeper so he'll leave us alone?"

"Not exactly. But he said maybe he can help us make it so the Gatekeeper leaves us alone, if . . ."

"If what, Daddy?"

"If you're strong enough to do a really hard thing."

Emma steeled herself. "What do I have to do?"

"That's the problem. We don't really know. We can bet it's not shooting the MacDonalds, but we don't know for sure what it is."

Emma's eyes fell. "Then how can I do it?"

Rob and Marcia exchanged a searching glance. Finally, Marcia responded to Emma's question. "We don't know for sure, sweetie. It's especially hard to know what to do, since none of us can really control the actions of the people we're inside of."

"I can," Emma nodded a little as she spoke. "I can control Mary Ellen now. The Gatekeeper let me do it because Mary Ellen doesn't do what he wants anyway."

The parents shared another look, with a new light in their eyes.

"But how can I do something, if I don't know what it is?"

Marcia straightened Emma's hair with gentle strokes. "Well, I guess you will just always have to be careful to do the best thing, no matter how hard it is. If you always think about it that way, when it comes time to do whatever you need to do, you'll know what it is. Just always do good."

Emma blinked. "I'll try, Mommy, but the Gatekeeper makes it hard. He always wants me to do things that aren't good. And sometimes I'm afraid not to do what he says."

Rob took her hand. "Don't be afraid. I know it's hard, but if you aren't afraid, he can't make you do things you don't want to do—things that are bad."

Emma attempted a smile. "I'll try, but it's hard not to be afraid."

Her failed smile forced her father to close his eyes and purse his lips. He swallowed hard.

"I know. I know it is. But you're the only one of us who can." He turned toward his wife. "She's just a child. It's so unfair to put this all on her."

Marcia took their clasped hands into her own. "Emma, listen to me. It will be all right. We are always with you. Don't be afraid. Listen to your heart. Follow it, not the Gatekeeper. If you do that, we'll all be okay."

Emma met her gaze with eyes searching for confidence. "I will, Mommy. I will."

They hugged each other in silence for a long time. At last, Rob said, "Well, I guess we should probably call the nurse. They'll want to know she's awake."

"Let them wait," Marcia said. "They'll want to climb all over her. And they won't figure out any more than they know now. All that can wait a few minutes longer. We know there's nothing wrong with her, and I'm not done hugging my baby yet."

Chapter 31

"Daddy, what did the doctors say was wrong with me when I was in the hospital?" Emma sat on the couch, snuggled under her father's arm as they watched TV.

"They never really found out."

"They don't know about the Gatekeeper?"

"No. Only you and I and Mommy know about him."

"You didn't tell the doctor the Gatekeeper made me sick?"

"No. I didn't tell them."

"Why not?"

Rob sighed. "Well, for one thing, they wouldn't have understood what I was talking about. I'm sure they've never been to the other place. So they probably wouldn't have believed me. It's pretty weird going to the same place every time you fall asleep. They would have thought I sounded crazy."

"You're not crazy, Daddy. But I guess it's good you didn't tell them."

"They'll just have to go on believing it's a medical mystery."

"What's a medical mystery?"

"That's when somebody gets sick and the doctors can't figure out why."

"And then the person gets better again?"

"Sometimes."

"Am I better again?"

"Sure you are. You feel better, don't you?"

"Yeah." She nuzzled herself closer to him. "Do you think it will happen again?"

"No. I don't think so."

"Why not?"

"Because the Gatekeeper has no reason to do it to you now. We know his secret."

She accepted this and was quiet for a minute.

"Daddy, do you think we'll ever get rid of the Gatekeeper?" There was more curiosity in her voice than fear.

"Yes."

"How?"

"I'm not sure yet, but we will."

"He'll leave us alone if I shoot Mary Ellen's parents. He said so."

Rob looked down at her and shook his head. "You can't do that."

"Why? If it's just a dream, then nobody will really get shot."

"Because it's not. . ." He was about to say it wasn't a dream, but believing it was only a dream could be the biggest thing helping her manage her fear. "It's not right to do bad things, even in dreams."

"But then we could just forget about it. You always tell me to forget about my bad dreams."

He gave her a little squeeze. "I know I do, but this is different."

"How?"

"You may not be able to forget this one so easily. If you shoot somebody in this dream, you may remember it for a long time, and I don't want you to have to hold onto that memory."

She nodded. "I do remember this dream a lot better than other bad dreams I've had."

"That's why we have to get rid of it in the right way, without making it worse. Remember what Mommy and I told you. Always do what feels like it will do the most good for everyone, even if it's hard, and it will work out all right."

"I'm so sick of this dream, and I'm so sick of the Gatekeeper. I think I'd do anything to be left alone. Sometimes I think I should just do what he wants and shoot them. Then it would be all over and he'd leave me alone." She looked up at him, almost beseechingly. "And it would be all over for you and Mommy, too."

She had no idea how right she was about that.

176

Chapter 32

Dan McGillivray's automobile was a much earlier model than the one Whidden and Carroll had arrived in. Some of the repairs had been done using homemade parts, not intended for use on such a machine. As a result, it sputtered and made sundry noises unique to itself among the growing number of autos in the province.

The noise of McGillivray's automobile brought Alex from the house. As Janet and Mary Ellen exited the vehicle, Alex went around and thanked the driver for his hospitality.

"I got a telephone call from the Halifax Herold," McGillivray told him. "Looking for one of their men, fellow named Whidden. Janet says he's up here with you."

Alex nodded. "He's in the house."

"They want him to telephone. Been trying to get hold of him all night. Called all over town before they got me."

"I'll tell him."

"If he can come now, I'll drive him to my place. He can put his call through from my telephone."

"Janet," Alex shouted over the car. "Go inside and tell Mr. Whidden he's wanted outside." Janet and Mary Ellen hurried to the house.

McGillivray made conversation as they waited for Whidden. "How long you suppose it will be before they run telephone lines out here?"

Alex shrugged. "Don't much matter anyhow. We got no need of a telephone."

McGillivray chuckled. "We used to think that way too. But now the wife would faint dead if you took the telephone away. Same with electric lights and this old beauty." He patted the steering wheel.

"Never thought I needed 'em, 'til I got 'em. Now I'd be hard pressed to live without 'em."

"I reckon I'll stay happy in my ignorance then," Alex said.

"Ignorance is bliss. Isn't that what they say?"

Alex shrugged again. "Don't know what they say, Dan, but I know what I need and what I don't."

Janet and Whidden appeared from the house. When they came near, McGillivray told Whidden of the call for him and repeated his offer to drive him to the telephone.

Whidden looked over his shoulder at the MacDonald house and pursed his lips, weighing competing notions in his mind. "Well," he said at last, "I hate to leave just now, but I suppose it must be important if they went to such lengths to find me. I'd better see what they want. I'll come back as soon as I can."

He got into the automobile. The driver waved to the MacDonalds, turned the car around, and drove off in the direction from which he'd come.

Mr. and Mrs. MacDonald watched them go. "That leaves one," Alex said, nodding to where Carroll's auto was parked. "I wish we could be rid of that one too, and get back to our old lives."

Janet cautiously raised her gaze to meet his eyes, measuring the right time to ask the question on her mind. "While we were gone," she began, "were there any—did anything happen?"

"Lots happened," he replied, letting his eyes escape her gaze, "but no, there weren't no fires."

She turned her head away from him. "I almost wished I'd find the whole place burned down. I'd just as soon it was burned to the ground if it would show them she's a good girl."

He didn't say anything, and he didn't look at her, but he stepped close to her and took her hand. He held it for just a moment before letting go. Then they walked toward the house together, but not touching, like a respectable married couple.

As they rounded the corner of the house they came upon Dr. Prince. There could be no reason for his lurking there other than he was waiting for them, out of sight of Whidden. He drew himself up as they came face to face with him, looking into each of their faces meaningfully.

"What is it, Dr. Prince?" Janet asked. "Is something wrong?"

"In a word, yes."

"Is Mary Ellen all right? Surely, nothing could have happened in the few minutes we've been back."

"Mary Ellen is far from all right. I need you both to understand that." He tilted his head toward the corner the MacDonalds had just walked around. "These men have no business here. They're wasting our time, and our time is short and precious. They've wasted too much of it already. I'm afraid I just can't do enough for your daughter in the time I have left here."

"Are you leaving?" Alex asked.

"I must go soon, and we've made too little progress with Mary Ellen."

"What should we do?" Janet asked.

"Well, since I have not been able to convince you to punish her bad behavior as sternly as is necessary, and since I have run short of time in which to convince you of that necessity, I'm afraid the only solution that remains is to institutionalize her."

Both parents' heads fell as they each took an unsteady step backward. "The asylum?" Janet asked sheepishly.

"I have connections. I can get her into an excellent facility where they'll treat her kindly."

Janet straightened herself, reclaiming the step she had retreated. "No. I won't allow it. She's our daughter and she's best here with us."

Her words bounced off Dr. Prince. She was too firm in her emotions and could not be swayed by logical argument. He ignored her and turned his words toward Alex. "She'll kill you all, or you'll kill her first."

"No," Alex replied. "She wouldn't. We wouldn't."

"Wouldn't she? She's already tried, more than once."

"But you said it's not really her. She doesn't mean to do it."

"Will that matter to you when you're all burnt to death?"

"I'll stop her," Alex promised. "I'll give her such whippings as she'll be sure to know it has to stop, just like you want me to."

"Ah, but you won't," Dr. Prince countered. "You'll mean to, but something will make you go soft." He gave a meaningful look at Janet. "You'll slack off on the correction and things will get worse. They'll get worse until you're all burnt up. Or maybe one day your vexation at the fires will overpower you, and you'll overcompensate for all the lax punishments and beat the girl to death."

Alex sucked in a large, aggrieved breath. "I would never!"

Dr. Prince issued a sigh that was perhaps meant to calm Alex. "Of course you would never. You would never mean to do it. In all the cases I've seen, no one ever meant to do it. But that doesn't change the many times it's happened. I'm afraid I've seen it before, all too often."

The husband and wife exchanged a searching glance. "No," Janet said. "He would never do lasting harm to Mary Ellen. He's her father and he loves her as much as any father loves his child."

Dr. Prince gave a little shake of his head. "I know you believe that, and it's right that you do. I know you also believe that Mary Ellen would never do you any serious harm. But you must believe me. I've seen too many of these sorts of things not to know better. If things go on as they are here, it will not end well for any of you. With the heart of my expertise, I can promise you that." Delivering this verdict, he looked forcefully into Alex's eyes.

Alex's resolved cracked under the doctor's gaze. "Would they treat her well in the asylum? Would they be kind and look after all her needs?"

The doctor gave him a reassuring smile. "Of course, they would. I would only send her to the most modern and enlightened of facilities. They'd have everything they need to look after her, make her comfortable, and help her through her difficulties. They have experience with girls like her. As much as you love her, you lack that experience, and that is the key to making her well again."

Now it was Janet's turn to stare fiercely at Alex. "She needs to be with her family. Love is more powerful than all their science. No one can care for her better than her parents."

Alex said nothing. Instead, he showed the doctor an expression indicating his reluctance to contradict his wife's position.

Dr. Prince closed his eyes and clenched his teeth just long enough to calm his temper. "I can see you are not ready to believe me. I'll let it drop for now. But will you do me the favor of taking some time to discuss it between yourselves? Take a stroll together through this beautiful landscape and ask yourselves if you are truly ready for what is yet to come, because what's to come is ten times worse than anything you've seen yet. Will you do that much?"

"What about Mary Ellen?" Janet asked.

"She's in the house," Dr. Prince replied. "I'll look after her until you get back, and make sure there's no trouble while you're gone."

Janet's face grew long. "I don't like to leave her with a stranger."

"I hardly think I'm a stranger," Dr. Prince replied, brushing aside any show of offense he might have rightfully made. "Mary Ellen and I have quite friendly conversations. I'm only asking you to take a brief moment for serious contemplation on an issue of the greatest importance to your family."

Alex turned to his wife. "It'll be all right," he told her. "It's only for a little while."

Janet addressed Dr. Prince. "You won't mention any of this asylum talk to her, will you?"

Dr. Prince shook his head and waved his hand to reassure her. "Of course not. This sort of information must come only from those she loves and trusts most."

Alex took Janet's hand and led her away. Janet threw several glances over her shoulder toward Dr. Prince before he disappeared into the house.

"Are you persuaded we should send her away?" Janet asked her husband as they walked.

"I don't like the idea. But suppose what he says is true? What if things only get worse?"

"If they do, then so be it. I'm with our little girl, come what may. If my faith in her costs me everything I have, then that's the way it was meant to be. I'll do anything for her except let them take her away from her parents."

"Even if it costs our lives, or hers?"

"Even so."

"And that's your true feeling?"

"It is."

"Then we're agreed."

Janet squeezed his hand and smiled into his face. "Let's go tell Dr. Prince."

He held her back. "Wait a while. If we go back too soon, he'll think we decided in haste. Let's walk a while before we go back. Maybe he'll drop it for good if he thinks we talked on it for a good long while."

They walked on in silence.

Chapter 33

Mary Ellen took refuge in her parents' room. With her parents outside talking to Whidden and McGillivray, she feared she was left alone in the house with Dr. Prince, and she didn't like that. She wasn't sure if Dr. Prince were in the house or not, so it was safest to stay in her parents' room until she heard her mother or father come in. She didn't know where Detective Carroll was. In any case, she decided she couldn't count on him for protection. She didn't know anything about him, and she couldn't assume he wasn't just as bad as Dr. Prince.

She'd wait here until her parents came in, lying on the bed with her face buried in her arms. If it were left up to her, she'd just wait here until Dr. Prince left, however long that would be. She figured she could stay in this room for days on end if it meant avoiding him. But she knew her parents wouldn't let her. Dr. Prince was a very important man who had come a long way to see her. It would be an embarrassment to the family to have her hide from him until he left. She would have to face him again. Her best hope was to avoid being left alone with him.

She heard McGillivray's car drive away. She hoped this meant her parents would come inside, but though she perked up her ears listening for their voices, she heard nothing of them inside the house. After what seemed a long time of waiting, she heard the back door open and close. A few seconds later, the bedroom door swung open. Good, she thought, one of her parents had come to her. The door closed again. There was something in that sound of the bedroom door closing that told her it was not a parent that came in. Mary Ellen raised her head out of her arms, knowing who she would see in the room with her.

He stepped to the foot of the bed and stopped. "It's so nice to be home again, isn't it? No doubt, the McGillivrays are good hosts, but it always feels good to be home."

Mary Ellen sat up and put her feet over the side of the bed, searching for the first opportunity to flee.

"That's fine," he said. "You needn't say much. I only need to know if you're ready to do your duty." He bent closer and stared hard into her face. "You, inside there, Emma, are you ready?"

Mary Ellen shook her head.

Where annoyance or even rage might have been expected from him, there came resignation. "Very well, then. I see I can do nothing with you. It's very disappointing, but I'm afraid I must admit defeat. You've outlasted me."

Mary Ellen's eyes scanned his face, searching for some cause of his sudden change in demeanor.

"I've tried to settle this business here in your own home, but unfortunately, you have refused to cooperate at every turn. There needs to be a change made. Therefore, your parents have decided to institutionalize you."

Mary Ellen's eyes grew wide. She slid away from him along the edge of the bed.

Dr. Prince took a few steps closer. "Mary Ellen doesn't know what that means. The asylum is all in the future for her." He leaned forward, bracing himself with hands on knees, bringing himself lower to stare into the girl's eyes. "But Emma knows. Emma's seen it. Haven't you Emma? Remember the little room with no windows? The man with the clipboard? All those unpleasant questions he asked?"

He nodded satisfaction to himself, waiting to see if Emma would show any reaction through Mary Ellen.

"Yes, Emma knows the horrors of the asylum. That's what's in store for you after the next fire, and you know there will be a next fire, don't you?" He rubbed his lips together as though savoring some pleasant taste.

"I don't know any such thing." It was Emma's thought, but Mary Ellen's mouth spoke it.

"Ah, well. You aren't cured, and I have to go away, so it only stands to reason there will be another fire. And when there is, your parents, Mr. and Mrs. MacDonald that is, will certainly send you to the asylum and be done with you for good. You will live in a little, dark room and they will go on with their lives as if you never existed."

He straightened himself up, reached into his jacket pocket, and extracted the revolver just enough to make Emma understand. "Unless you are brave enough to take that evil choice away from them."

Mary Ellen shivered. She scooted herself across the bed, away from him.

Dr. Prince shrugged and shook his head a little. "Suit yourself. I've done everything I can to help you avoid the miserable future they have in store for you. I can do no more. You want me to go away for good?"

She nodded.

"Very well. Then there is just one little thing you must do." From behind his back he produced a rolled-up paper. It resembled a long funnel, with the bottom rolled to a tight point. Even scrunched up as it was, she could see that it was covered with writing.

"Here are my instructions in this matter. I would let you read them, but I believe you haven't learned to read yet." He peered deep into her eyes. "Isn't that right, Emma?"

She remained perfectly still. The Gatekeeper knew very well she understood written words when Mary Ellen's eyes read them to her. He was making fun of her.

With his free hand, he reached into his pocket and brought forth a matchstick. "All you have to do is burn these instructions, and I will disappear. Poof! Just like that."

She didn't believe him. He was a liar.

He held out both objects toward her. "Here. What have you got to lose? You can send me away right now."

She would not put out her hands.

"Afraid of a little fire?" he mocked. "I'd think this little bit of paper would be nothing for you to burn. You're so good at burning things."

Her only reply was to squint at him and push her lips together hard.

"Ah. Well. I can't waste time with such a bump on a log. I really thought you had more spirit than that. Suit yourself." He lay the rolled paper and the matchstick at the foot of the bed. Then he opened the door, passed through, and closed it again, making sure he was not seen leaving the room, in case her parents had already come back into the house.

Emma stared at the items he'd left. It was Mary Ellen's body, but the Gatekeeper had given Emma control over it. It was for Emma to decide what to do next, and it was a difficult decision.

On the one hand, the Gatekeeper couldn't be trusted. He was the kind of man who told lies and then joked about it. He was mean to little girls and tried to make them do bad things. He was trying to make her start a fire right now.

But then, even a serial liar could tell the truth once in a while. Emma picked up the paper and teased apart some of the wrinkles at the top, where the pages weren't wound up so tightly. Mary Ellen's eyes could read it to her. At least she could figure out if it were his instructions, like he said. That would give her a clue.

There was writing on the paper, but Mary Ellen's eyes couldn't read it. It was a trail of strange characters. They were foreign and creepy looking, just like the Gatekeeper's instructions would be. Mary Ellen's reading skills would be no help.

This odd writing confused Emma even more. The queer symbols made it seem like this paper was what he said it was. Yet the fact that he gave her something Mary Ellen couldn't read lent suspicion. If these really were his instructions, then burning them could really be the end of it. She didn't know if these things worked that way, but they might.

She convinced herself there was a certain logic behind it. The Gatekeeper realized Emma wouldn't shoot people and was sick and tired of trying to make her do it. She wouldn't have trusted that happy conclusion, except that her parents told her she must do something very difficult. After all she had seen and experienced here, she could think of nothing more difficult than starting a fire. She didn't even like being near matches. The thought of striking one made her tremble.

It all kind of made sense, now that she thought of it. After all this time of being made terrified of fire, she had to burn something herself. That was the hard thing she had to do. She doubted she was brave enough to do it, but then she thought of her parents, and that gave her courage.

There was an empty porcelain basin on the bureau. That would provide some safety. Once she got the paper burning good, she'd drop it in the basin. If she were careful, she wouldn't get burned and nothing else would catch fire. Even if it were all a lie, there would be no harm in testing it.

She picked up the matchstick. Her hand shook. There was some difference between thinking it would be all right to do and actually doing it. It meant lighting a fire, and even lighting a little fire was the last thing she wanted to do these days. But she had been warned it would be difficult. Getting rid of the Gatekeeper meant doing the hard thing.

Emma had only ever struck the couple of matches the Gatekeeper had made her strike. She was not good at it, but Mary Ellen had spent much of her life lighting kerosene lamps and cooking stoves. If it were a good match, it would be a simple matter of striking it against the sole of her shoe. Then she could light the paper and go set it in the basin.

She had better do it quickly before everyone came into the house, and before they started looking for her. She struck the match. Holding her hand as still as possible she held the match to the top edge of the paper. The paper began to burn, but it burned slowly and unreliably. It looked as though it might even extinguish itself without being damaged much at all. She blew out the match before it burned down to her fingers.

The paper burned feebly at the places she had lit it. Some of the spots burned out. The few remaining promised to follow suit very soon. Emma didn't know fire doesn't like to burn downward. Mary Ellen knew. It was the sort of thing someone of her upbringing would learn early. Before the fire burnt out, Emma understood her mistake. She slowly turned the funnel of paper upside down. As she turned it, the flames revived. They reached upward into the funnel.

In the seconds before the funnel was completely overturned, she noticed something strange. A grayish sand began to trickle down the inside of the funnel. She had no time to wonder what this strange powder might be before it contacted the growing flame.

A bright flash of flame and heat made her scream and cast the paper from her hand. The funnel disintegrated into numerous burning bits, falling onto the bed and floor all around. After the first shock wore off, she felt a sharp stinging in her hand. Her palm was dark red and it stung with hot pain.

Janet burst through the door, Alex on her heels. "Mary Ellen!" Janet cried, rushing to rescue her girl from the ring of fire.

Alex grimaced and said nothing as he hurried to extinguish the various bits of burning debris by rolling up the bedspread on them.

The fires were more frightening than dangerous. Little bits of burning paper and scorched bed coverings were not difficult to put out. The danger lay in what came next.

All three MacDonalds were drawn away from their immediate troubles by the sound of tapping in the doorway. Together, they looked toward the sound and were rewarded with the sight of Dr. Prince standing there. In his right hand he held his rattan cane, which he was tapping on the floor. Despite the troubling circumstances, he wore a faint, condescending smile on his face.

He addressed his first words to Alex. "Are you through doubting me now?" He did not wait for an answer. "You saw it for yourselves this time, didn't you? The child was alone, busying herself with setting her own parents' bedroom on fire. Is this enough for you? Perhaps you will be convinced to trust in my advice now." He tapped the end of the cane down one last time with greater force.

All eyes fell to the cane. Alex's shoulders drooped. Janet bowed her head.

Instead of hiding behind her mother, as she would previously have done, Mary Ellen stood apart. She was the most upright of all the MacDonalds. Her attitude was no longer a reflection of the old, persecuted Mary Ellen, but the new, angry Emma.

She raised her arm, pointing her finger directly into esteemed doctor's face. "You tricked me! You're a liar!"

Dr. Prince smirked. "Impudence. Well, at least that's not as dangerous as arson."

"Mary Ellen! Shush!" Janet attempted to pull her daughter to her, away from the brink of this shocking rudeness.

Emma swam free of her. "I'm not Mary Ellen. I'm Emma." She reasserted her pointing denouncement of their guest. "And he's not any doctor. He's the Gatekeeper."

Dr. Prince shook his head and made noises with his tongue and teeth. "I feared as much. Too much time has been wasted. She's more delusional than ever." He looked pointedly at Alex. "If only you had followed my instructions from the first. It might not have gone this far."

"This far?" Alex muttered.

"You heard it yourself!" Dr. Prince replied. "My God, man, I tried to warn you! She won't even acknowledge her given name. She's created an alternate personality to cast all the blame onto. And now this alternate personality is taking her over. Is this what you wanted?"

Alex looked at the floor and shook his head.

"Well then, let's do something about it. Bring her out." Dr. Prince turned and walked out to the front room.

Alex looked hard at Janet. He led her eyes with his own to the rolled-up bedspread. Then he took his eyes back to hers and let them rest there until they elicited an almost imperceptible nod from her.

Chapter 34

Alex pulled the reluctant Mary Ellen from the bedroom. She resisted, shouting odd and disturbing statements. "He's tricking you," she yelled. "He's not the real Dr. Prince. He tricked me into burning the papers and now he's tricking you into punishing me!"

None of her babble made any sense to Alex. It made perfect sense to Rob, but in the heat of the moment, his struggle to moderate Alex's temper was inadequate. Rob could not make Alex see how she could be tricked into setting fires or why her parents would need to be tricked into disciplining her.

Alex dragged Mary Ellen to the front room. "Be quiet, girl. You brought this on yourself."

"No! He made me do it! He always made me do it!"

Alex's reply was swift. His hand struck the girl across the face. "I said quiet, and I mean it!"

The shock of the blow went deep. Emma had experienced Mary Ellen's punishment before, but this blow came unannounced, and it hurt. The pain transcended Mary Ellen and flowed through Emma. It left Emma stunned.

There was no more resistance from the girl. The only sounds from her mouth were pitiful sobs. Alex had made his point; protest would not serve her well.

Dr. Prince waited for them in the front room. Detective Carroll was with him. This gave Marcia and Rob a flicker of hope. If they had no power to prevent the MacDonalds from caning their child, surely the law did.

"I was just explaining the situation to Detective Carroll," Dr. Prince said to Alex and Janet. "It's a bit of luck such a respected law officer is here. This way there can be no insinuation that you beat your child wantonly. Let it be a comfort to you that he understands the severity of the child's latest mischief and can attest that stern punishment is warranted."

Detective Carroll gave them a single, severe nod as sanction from the law to proceed under Dr. Prince's guidance. Together, the hopes of Marcia and Rob wilted.

Dr. Prince stepped forward and held out his rattan cane to Alex. "No half measures," he insisted. "You must be firm and follow through. If you show any weakness, you stand to lose her for good."

Alex took the cane in tentative hands.

"The more pain you elicit today, the less she will endure in the future. You understand?"

Alex nodded a short, indecisive nod.

The nod was unsatisfactory to Dr. Prince. "Do you?" he asked again.

"Yes." The quiet word was nearly inaudible.

"Then hold the cane firmly. Hold it like a man determined to save his family."

Alex tightened his grip on the cane.

Dr. Prince smiled. "Now we understand each other."

Chapter 35

When Alex took hold of the cane, Mary Ellen shrunk away from him. She retreated to the door leading outside of the house. Defying all of Rob's will power, Alex stepped toward her. Against Marcia's will, Janet did nothing to hold him back. Even the mother could not raise a defense in the face of overwhelming evidence.

Now, as the parents' determination to dole out harsh punishment gained momentum, an unlikely force held it back. Dr. Prince put a hand on Alex's arm. "One moment." Looking into Alex's confused eyes, he explained. "There must be a clear connection between the crime and the punishment. She must know exactly why she is being punished and what is to be expected of her hereafter. Otherwise the punishment will do no good." A strange light came into his eyes. "I have great experience in this. Allow me a moment with her; there must be no confusion about what is going to happen now."

Alex relaxed his grip on the cane and shrugged. Of course he would do whatever Dr. Prince asked. He had lost control of events, and anyone who spoke to him stridently would exert their will over him. Dr. Prince acknowledged his obedience with a smile.

The doctor crossed to where Mary Ellen cowered before the door. He bent over and took her chin into his hand. He pointed her eyes at him and grinned. Whispering so that none might overhear, he told her, "Your time has come, my dear. This is your moment."

Mary Ellen stared at him with blank eyes, and Emma said nothing, wary that every time she spoke, she made things worse for herself.

Dr. Prince licked his lips. "I see you are prepared to listen now. That's very good. Listen well. You see they are determined to beat you now, both of them. Have you ever been beaten with a rattan cane? No? Well, let me tell you, it is not pleasant. It will hurt more than anything you have felt before. And when I say this, I am talking to you Emma. You hardly felt the punishments before, but this time you will feel every bit of it. And I assure you, you will never be the same."

"What can you do?" Dr. Prince puffed out his lower lip as if it were a sympathetic question. "You can be beaten until you are sure your parents despise you. You can yell at them ridiculous statements they won't understand." He spread out the palms of his hands as invitation. "Go ahead. Try it. Tell them I'm trying to make you shoot them. They'll only beat you harder, and the policeman will take you to the crazy house to boot."

It was taking a long time for Dr. Prince to explain things to Mary Ellen. Janet gave Alex a hard look. In her eyes, Marcia pleaded with Rob to do something to make Alex turn against Dr. Prince. In the reply look Alex gave, Rob strained to express that every ounce of his energy was being employed to do just that.

Dr. Prince shook his head mournfully at Mary Ellen. "What are you to do then?" He grinned again as he reached into the inside pocket of his suit jacket. Shielded by his body so no one else could see it, he produced his small revolver. "End it without pain. It will be so easy, and then it will all be over."

"I can't." Emma's voice was soft and unsteady. "I don't know how to shoot it."

Dr. Prince chuckled without noise. "Don't worry. Mary Ellen is a country girl. She knows how to do it. I bet she's a fair marksman too. All you have to do is make the choice to do your duty. Tell her body to do it; she will take it from there."

Emma looked at him with forlorn eyes. A tear rolled down Mary Ellen's cheek. This only made Dr. Prince grin. The Gatekeeper liked sad tears. They were his stock and trade. Besides, it showed that the girl's resolve was cracking. He was winning.

"We can't wait forever. I can't stall the beating much longer." Keeping the action blocked from view with his body, Dr. Prince pushed the revolver toward her. "Take it."

The girl took a deep breath and stiffened her form. "No. I won't."

Dr. Prince's grin turned to a sneer. He huffed an exasperated breath. "I'm getting tired of waiting for you, little girl. I might have waited longer, but that baby in your Mama's belly forced my hand. Now we are at the critical moment whether we like it or not. You must choose now. If you don't, I'll take that baby, and then we'll start all over again from the beginning. Do you want to go through this all over again? Do you want your baby brother to die?"

Even as he hissed this last question, Dr. Prince stared over his shoulder at Janet MacDonald. She let out a cry of pain, hunched forward, and grabbed her belly.

Chapter 36

Marcia felt a dim pain. It wasn't much, not like what Janet must be feeling to make her double up as she did. Yet, it didn't take much pain to make Marcia think of the baby. This odd world, ruled by an evil that stole children from their sleep, was no place for her baby. It was no place for her little girl, or any of them. She had to get them out of here and the only tool she had available was Janet.

She forced herself to stop thinking of her baby. She had to focus on Janet now. She had to gain control.

Alex put his arm around Janet to stop her from falling. "What's wrong?"

Janet straightened herself, embarrassed that the men had seen her lurch. "It's okay now. I just had a bit of pain on my insides. It's just worry about Mary Ellen that has my insides tied up in knots. I'll be fine."

Marcia strained to focus her thoughts toward Janet. "Tell him not to go through with it!" she wished at Janet. "Tell him it's killing you to see this! He'll stop it for you." She tried to move Janet's mouth to say these things, but her will wasn't strong enough.

"Well then, the sooner it's finished the better." Alex let go of Janet and took a step toward Dr. Prince and his daughter.

Rob strained every bit of his will power to hold Alex back. His mind screamed, "Stop! Don't you see what you're doing? You'll beat her black and blue and nothing will change, except maybe she'll be crippled. Is that what you want?" It was no use. He wasn't strong enough yet in this world to exert control over the farmer.

Dr. Prince held up his hand as Alex approached. "Allow me just one moment more with girl, if you please."

Alex fidgeted. "We'll want to get this business over with, soon as we can. It don't do no good to drag it out."

Dr. Prince gave him an annoyed nod. "Yes. Of course. But the girl's understanding must be prepared first. Everything in its proper order."

Alex looked over his shoulder at Janet. She was upright again, apparently feeling better. She nodded at him to obey the doctor. Alex took a step backward.

Satisfied, Dr. Prince returned his attention to the girl. "Now then, sweetie, we are short on time. This is your last chance." He pushed the revolver at her again. "Take it. Do what's right, and do it quickly. Mary Ellen will do the hard part. All you have to do is tell her to do it."

"The right thing?" Emma said the question to herself as she fought off confusion. Wasn't saving Mommy's new baby the right thing? The girl reached out and touched the pistol.

Dr. Prince smiled reassurance. "There now. See? It's not that hard."

A thought leapt into Emma's mind. What if she shot him instead? That would certainly be better than shooting two good people.

Dr. Prince frowned. He could read the thought in her eyes. "You know what happens when you try to shoot at a little man who isn't there?"

The girl flinched before his fiery eyes.

"You can't kill a man who isn't there," Dr. Prince answered himself, "but you certainly can make him angry, very angry."

Janet cried out in pain and doubled over again.

Chapter 37

Alex stepped forward. "Dr. Prince, the strain weighs heavy on my wife. We can't wait."

"One moment more, I beg of you!" Dr. Prince fairly spit at him.

Alex stepped back. There was a tremor in his hands.

Dr. Prince turned back to the girl. "Now. The time is now."

The girl took hold of the revolver.

"When I step to the side, do your duty. You must shoot both of them, and quickly."

Emma had to do it. He'd kill the baby. She was the only one who could save it. She didn't want to shoot these people, but what choice did she have?

Mary Ellen held the revolver loosely in a shaking hand. This made Dr. Prince frown with doubt. "We must firm up your resolve a bit," he whispered to Emma. Over his shoulder he announced, "Mr. MacDonald, this child shows no remorse whatsoever, even in light of the beating she knows is coming to her. It won't be enough. You must tell her firmly that you have decided to send her to the asylum."

Alex's eyes widened. He stood in a stupor.

"There's no time to vacillate! Tell her now! It's the only thing left in this world that can save her!"

Alex's exhausted mind could resist no more. If it were the only thing that could save his daughter, then it must be done, despite the pain it would cause. He opened his mouth to speak.

"No! No!" Rob yelled at Alex from the inside. "The asylum will destroy her! For once in your life, don't rely on cold calculation! Follow you heart! It knows!"

Alex stopped what he was about to say. He straightened himself up tall on two firmly planted feet. "No. I won't send her there. I'd die first!"

Emma saw her own father in Alex's eyes more clearly than ever before. It was he who was speaking in Alex MacDonald's voice. This phenomenon brought revelation to her young mind and the terrible truth hit her. If the baby were causing Janet pain, then the baby must be inside Janet, and if the baby were inside her, so must be her own mother. Mary Ellen's parents were not merely dream people. To shoot the MacDonalds would be to kill her own parents.

Janet let out a terrible scream and clutched at her belly. Dr. Prince hissed at Emma in desperate words. "I'll take the real baby, and maybe your real mother will go with it too, if you don't shoot these fake people!"

Mary Ellen's hand closed around the pistol handle more firmly. Dr. Prince eyes showed hope, but he had revealed too much to Emma in his desperation. No one was fake here. They were all real. Shooting the MacDonalds was not the right thing, and she knew she must do the right thing. But then, she still couldn't see the right thing. She knew she must not shoot Mary Ellen's parents, and she could not shoot the Gatekeeper. The only other person was the policeman, but it made no sense to her that shooting him could be the right thing.

There was no one left to shoot.

Encouraged by Mary Ellen's determined grip of the revolver, Dr. Prince stepped out from between the girl and her parents. They saw the revolver in her hand. Alex froze. Janet screamed.

The girl raised the pistol. There was someone else. Of course there was. It all made sense. The hardest thing, the right thing, the only way to save her parents for good and all.

She must do it quickly, before fear stole her resolve.

The most difficult thing—she understood it now. The confusion melted away, leaving only one certain path.

She pointed the pistol at herself and squeezed the trigger.

The door swung open and jarred her elbow as the weapon fired. The pistol flew into the air and the girl fell to the side. The report of the firearm, strange and shocking inside the house, stirred everyone to action. They were huddled around the girl in an instant, searching for blood, hoping for signs of life.

There was no blood. The bullet, redirected by the blow to the girl's elbow, had lodged harmlessly in the wall. The girl had no injury worse than a bruised arm.

Detective Carroll collected the pistol and helped the girl to her feet, keeping a firm hold on her all the while.

Satisfied the girl was unhurt, they turned their attentions to the doorway, in which stood the form of Mr. Whidden.

Whidden turned to the detective for answers. "What's going on here, Carroll? I was about to knock when I heard a scream. I rushed through the door and heard a gunshot. Who's shooting?"

Carroll held up the revolver. "The girl tried to kill herself. If you hadn't hit her arm coming through the door, she'd have done it, too."

Whidden let out a long, whistling breath. "It's a good thing I decided to wait on making that telephone call. I had that neighbor fellow let me out a ways down the road and walked back. Just in time too, by the looks of it."

"I daresay, you saved her life," Carroll explained.

"What now?" Whidden asked.

Though everyone had heard their discussion, Detective Carroll turned to make sure what he was about to say was told to all. "I'll have to take her into town. She's a danger to herself"—he lowered his voice—"and perhaps and danger to others."

Janet threw her arms around her daughter. "What will happen to her? Will they put her in jail?"

The detective's words came in as soft a tone as he could tell the hard truth in, but his hold on the girl's arm remained firm. "No. She won't go to jail. She'll go in for psychological evaluation. That will tell what's next. I'm sorry to have to say it, but she may have to be institutionalized for a while. Until it's clear she won't try to harm herself again."

"No! Don't take her away!" Janet pleaded. "I'll keep close watch on her. We both will. She wouldn't harm us, and we'll make sure she doesn't harm herself."

Dr. Prince reinserted himself at Carroll's elbow. "Perhaps her mother is right. It will be much easier for me to continue working with her here. All of my work with her will be lost if she's taken to an institution."

Carroll shook his head at them. "I'm sorry. As an officer of the law, there are certain things I can't ignore. A child attempting to take her own life is one of them. If I left this child here and she hurt someone, it would be on my hands, and rightly so. I'm afraid I have no choice." He addressed Janet specifically. "Would you mind packing some clothes for her? She may be away for some time."

Whidden stepped forward, as if to balance the presence of Dr. Prince. "Perhaps her mother could ride along into town with her? It would be a great comfort to them both, I imagine."

Carroll nodded. "There'd be no harm in that." He looked at Janet. "Go on now. Pack some things for the both of you. We'll have to leave directly."

Janet rushed off to the bedroom. Carroll led Mary Ellen to a chair. He relaxed his grip on her arm. "There. Sit down and keep still until your mother brings your things."

Mary Ellen obeyed, sitting and silently moving her confused eyes from person to person.

Carroll held the revolver out in front of Mary Ellen. "Now then, young lady. One thing I'd like to know is where you got this."

Mary Ellen turned her eyes toward Dr. Prince.

The doctor began patting his coat pockets as if searching for something. He glared at Mary Ellen. "She must have filched it from my pocket. It seems as though arson isn't her only criminal skill."

201

In a calm, firm voice Mary Ellen said, "He gave it to me."

Dr. Prince rolled his eyes at Carroll. "Ridiculous! The child is quickly becoming dangerously delusional. I suggest no delay in her evaluation."

"You always carry a revolver?" Carroll asked Dr. Prince.

"For personal protection. I never know when my investigations may lead me into the company of unsavory people."

Carroll put the revolver into his own pocket. "All right. Never mind. We'll get that all straightened out later."

Carroll turned to Whidden. "Will you be riding with us?"

Whidden had been studying Alex as the latter stood in silence. Alex had hardly moved since the firing of the weapon, and his eyes roamed in no less confused fashion than his daughter's did. "I think I'll stay behind for a while with Mr. MacDonald. He might like some company."

Whidden put a hand on Alex's shoulder and guided him to a chair. Alex allowed himself to be led as if he had no more faculty than one of his livestock.

They waited for Janet to return with an old carpet bag, puffed and straining with garments. Carroll reached out a hand to Mary Ellen. "We'd best get going."

Dr. Prince stepped forward again. "Since she's going, there's no point in my staying. I'd like to catch a lift with you, Detective. I'll just get my things."

Janet stiffened. The line of her shoulders straightened as though something long struggling within her had broken through a barrier. "Dr. Prince, I would be greatly obliged if you would consent to staying here with my husband tonight. It would be a great comfort to him and me both."

"Have no worries, Mrs. MacDonald," Dr. Prince replied. "Mr. Whidden has graciously offered to stay with your husband. And perhaps I can be of some further assistance to Mary Ellen. After all, I know her better than any of the other doctors who will examine her." He turned to mount the stairs in anticipation of retrieving his belongings.

Alex was up in an instant, grasping the doctor by the hand. A new clarity had taken hold of his confused eyes. He moved with a clear sense of purpose that was formerly beyond him. Speaking as if a new person had emerged within him, he said. "Dr. Prince, please. My wife is right. Your wisdom has done me a lot of good these past days. I'll need your wisdom more than ever tonight. You'll leave me bereft if you go now."

Dr. Prince pulled his hand free. "Mr. MacDonald, as you know, I took valuable time away from my business to come here and help your daughter. Now if there's any more chance for me to help her, as only I know how"—he rolled his eyes in an involuntary show of disgust—"I must remain at her side at all times, to guide her through the trials ahead."

As Dr. Prince climbed the stairs, Mr. and Mrs. MacDonald shared a glance. This look carried a form of communication heretofore foreign in their marriage. It was a clear understanding between partners of the actions each must take in order to assure the end they both sought. Their eyes met for just and instant before Alex turned to follow Dr. Prince upstairs, pleading for him to remain and getting in his way in a hundred different subtle actions.

As soon as they were out of sight, Janet MacDonald addressed Detective Carroll. "Sir, if you must take us away, you should do it quickly."

"What about Dr. Prince?" Carroll asked. "It sounds like he's still intent on coming along."

Whidden stepped forward, herding them toward the door. "Don't worry about him. I'll see he gets into town first thing tomorrow." He spoke to Janet. "Your husband has a horse cart, I assume."

"Of course."

"Perhaps we'll see you in town tomorrow, then." He gave Carroll a gentle push toward the door while Janet took Mary Ellen's hand

and led her in the same direction. "Good night, Detective. It may be best to let some of our fine Canadian doctors take over from here."

Carroll nodded. "I doubt they'd let an outside man near her, once I bring her in. Provincial regulations, you know."

"I think that's a relief to all of us." Whidden smiled at the MacDonald women. "Mrs. MacDonald, Mary Ellen, good luck. You'll always have my best wishes."

He closed the door behind them. From upstairs came the voices of Alex and Dr. Prince arguing, mingled with the creaking of the floorboards as Alex danced about, putting himself in the proper spots to cause Dr. Prince the utmost delay.

Whidden threw himself into a chair and let a satisfied smile cross his face as he listened past the uproar above for the sound of Carroll's motor car. At last, he thought he heard the faint sounds of it sneak past the upstairs noises. It faded away into the distance without prompting anyone to rush down and out the door after it. Whidden let out a sigh and closed his eyes. It was such great satisfaction. He'd had faith in her, of course, but she was still a very young child, after all. It would have been a very difficult thing to do for any human. Good thing the Gatekeeper had picked out such a strong girl. Through his closed eyes, Whidden still smiled.

Though none of the MacDonalds were in the room with him, Emma, Marcia, and Rob could see Whidden's smile. The three of them were no longer trapped within the bodies of Mary Ellen, Janet, and Alex. They stood, unseen, in the room, in same manner Emma had first stood with the Gatekeeper as Mary Ellen milked her cow. That had been the beginning of their family ordeal, and this was the end of it. Through the curiosity of what would happen next and the confusion of how they had been set free, they understood they were witnessing the end of their parts in the MacDonalds' story.

They watched Dr. Prince hurry down the stairs and pitch himself at the door, only to explode into a tirade of oaths as he realized he'd been left behind.

At last, Dr. Prince resigned himself to the situation and quieted down. He closed his mouth and stood still, considering. Then, he said to no one in particular, "I'm going to look for some coffee." He said this in a matter-of-fact tone as he turned and began toward the kitchen. Dr. Prince moved, and yet another man stood in the exact spot where he had been. It did not take Emma long to recognize the petite, dark-suited form of the Gatekeeper. In his left hand he held his felt hat.

The Gatekeeper scowled at Emma. There was anger and hatred in his eyes. He lifted his right hand and began to extend his index finger as if to wag it at her, but then he seemed to give up the notion altogether. His hand dropped to his side and he turned toward the door. He shuffled in a dejected manner, lifting his hat up to his head just before disappearing through the door without ever having opened it.

"I could have a cup of coffee, myself," Whidden said to the empty room. He rose from his chair and followed Dr. Prince into the kitchen. As he rose, another man remained seated in his chair. When Whidden had gone, this man rose as well. He was tall and well-kept. Rob thought he looked very much like an unusual plumber named Eli.

The man smiled at Rob's recognition of him. He smiled at Marcia too, but he smiled most brightly for Emma. He winked at the girl and gave her a thumbs up. Then he bowed slightly to them all and walked away in the opposite direction from the outside door. He disappeared through the rear wall.

It was light outside when Emma woke up in her parents' bed. She hugged them both at once. The daylight seemed brighter today. Maybe it was the knowledge that the nights would never be so dark again as they had been, now that none of them doubted they were done with the other place.

Chapter 38

Rob bounced the baby on his knee. Beside him, Marcia flipped through a month-old magazine. In the corner, Emma sorted through a collection of motley toys, searching for something interesting to occupy the time until they were called into the doctor's office.

Marica continued to flip pages without really looking at them. She watched Emma out of the corner of her eye. Even though things were better, it was difficult not to continue to worry now and then. "Do you think this will help her?" she asked her husband softly.

"Dr. Klavass is the most highly regarded child psychologist in the area," Rob replied. "I'm sure it won't hurt her to talk to him. And even if it doesn't help, I think she'll be all right in the long run."

"Do you think we're doing the right thing, though? It's all so unbelievable. I mean, that's why we were afraid to tell anybody before. Is it safe to tell anybody now? I don't want them to think she's got deep emotional problems."

"Things are different now that it's all over. She can tell it like it was a dream, just like we told her to. And they'll hear it like it was a dream. What else could they possibly think? She's a little girl who had some bad dreams—just like a million other little kids. They'll give her some strategies for feeling better about the dreams, and that will be that. With luck, those strategies will help her stop worrying about Mary Ellen."

"I hope you're right. I just get nervous about having her tell other people about it. I don't want there to be a stigma. I wouldn't even consider it if she didn't still talk about Mary Ellen so much."

"That's because she's a remarkably compassionate little girl. She formed a unique bond with Mary Ellen. It's only natural that she wonders about her. Don't you wonder about her too? And Janet and Alex?"

"Of course I do. But she worries about Mary Ellen too much. I don't want it to become an obsession with her. It's unsettling."

Rob cradled Baby Charlie in his arms. "Well, look at this way. None of us are involved in it anymore. That's a huge improvement. She gets to sleep at night, and if she dreams about Mary Ellen, which she's only done a few times, it's really a dream and nothing more. She's getting over a pretty big trauma, and she's doing a good job of it."

"I know. I just wish I could tell her something good about Mary Ellen so she wouldn't worry about her so much."

Rob nodded. "I wish you could too. But you can't lie to her. Eventually she'll be old enough to research it all herself. She'll learn the truth, so she might as well have it now. History is history, and none of it changed."

Marcia shook her head in remorse. "I know. I've read about her over a dozen times in the last six months, every time hoping it would somehow be better, that I would stumble upon some little happy nugget I overlooked before. It's no wonder Emma seems obsessed with it when I can't let it go either."

"It's natural, I suppose. We all had a strange sort of bond with her. Emma was practically part of her. We all want a happy ending for her."

Marcia raised her eyes to his. "Do you think about her too?"

"Sometimes. I mean, for a while she was my own daughter."

Marcia sighed. "Maybe we all need to see a psychologist."

"Maybe. Or maybe we all need to realize we didn't cause any of this. It happened a hundred years ago. How we got sucked into all of it will always be a puzzle, but Mary Ellen MacDonald's story was what it was before we even knew a single thing about it."

"I just wish there was some way we could have made it better."

He held her eyes level with his own. "How can you be sure we didn't? It's impossible to know one way or the other, but it seems like it could have been worse."

The inner office door swung open. A lady appeared from within. "Please come inside, all of you, and have a seat." Rob put the baby into his car seat. Marcia motioned to Emma to join them. Together, they followed the lady into a large room with tall windows in one wall. A couch and some comfortable chairs made a semicircle in the middle of the room. The lady waved her hand toward this area. "Sit wherever you'd like. Would anyone like some coffee or water?"

They all shook their heads. "No thank you," Marcia answered for all.

"Very well. It will only be a moment." She went out and closed the door behind her.

They sat together on the couch, Emma between her parents. Rob set the car seat on the carpet and rocked it with his foot, letting out a barely audible whistle as he surveyed the room. "This is a pretty posh setup. I guess it really pays to be a highly recommended child psychologist."

"I imagine it does, though I can't say from personal experience," answered a man's voice behind them.

They all turned around and followed the man with wide eyes as he walked past them and turned to face the place where they sat.

"Oh no!" Marcia breathed to herself.

Rob stirred himself, reaching for the handle of the baby's car seat as he began to rise from the couch.

The man extended a hand, urging calm upon all of them. "Please, don't run away. I promise you, I'm here to help."

"You're not Dr. Klavass," Marcia said in a soft, dispirited tone.

The man shook his head gently. "No, I'm not. As it happens, I'm not a plumber or a newspaper man either. But I think perhaps you know that already."

"Where's Klavass?" Rob demanded.

"I believe he's out of town this week."

"But we made this appointment weeks ago."

"You made an appointment, but it was not with Dr. Klavass. In your case, he and his staff were co-opted by higher powers."

Marcia leaned forward and pleaded with her hands. "Can't you all just leave us alone?"

The man looked squarely at her. "We can, and we will. This is the last time you will see me. If you will hear me out, I think it will benefit you all significantly more than any number of visits to even the best of doctors. Dr. Klavass is quite skilled, as I understand it, but he could never understand your situation the way I do. At the very least, I can save you a fair amount of doctor's bills. Is that acceptable to you?"

Both parents looked at Emma. She nodded to them both.

"I take that as a yes," the man said. "Does anyone mind if I sit down? That might be more comfortable for everyone." No one objected and the man sat in a chair facing the couch.

"Who are you?" Marcia asked.

The man pursed his lips for a second before saying, "That would be too difficult to explain. I don't even know how I would begin to make you understand. What you need to know is I am a friend. I think I've given you some evidence of that already."

They gave him subtle nods.

"Good. I hope I have earned some of your trust. It will help you if you trust what I tell you." They did nothing to indicate opposition to his statement, so he continued. "Now that the introductions, even though they must seem inadequate to you, are over, we may proceed to the meat of our discussion. The peace you hoped to reclaim in your lives is hindered by your concerns for the fate of Mary Ellen MacDonald. Yes. Well. This much I can tell you. Because of your efforts, and especially those of this brave little girl"—he nodded toward Emma—"Mary Ellen's life was no worse than it would have been."

"But it was no better, either?" Marcia asked.

"Well, no," the man replied. "But that was not the issue."

Marcia held up her palms. "What was the issue?"

The man crossed his legs and leaned back into his chair. "Let me see how well I can explain. Keep in mind, there are things I am not permitted to reveal to you, and there are things I do tell you that you may not understand perfectly. It is not intended that you understand them perfectly."

He scanned their faces to make sure they accepted this premise.

"Anyhow, let us begin with this. All things that occur in this world are meant to run to an ultimate purpose. Some of those things are happy things and some are sad things. But as long as they are working toward the intended purpose, they are all what you could call good things. Even tragic things are good, if they occur for their intended purpose."

The man shifted in his chair. Both Rob and Marcia eased back into the cushions of the couch.

"Opposed to this system are forces that would upset the ultimate purpose of events. Human beings, for natural reasons, tend to think of evil in terms of sad or painful events. Though these sorts of things are sometimes caused by evil, it is not necessarily so. Sometimes these events serve the greater purpose and are therefore good. The converse is true for happy events. Remember, not everything happy is good, and not everything mournful is evil."

The man leaned slightly forward. "My job, to use a familiar term, is to help events stay on track toward their intended purpose."

"They wouldn't on their own?" Rob asked.

"They would, if it weren't for the interference of entities whose sole purpose is to derail them from that track."

"Why would anyone do that?" Marcia asked.

"Because they are the root of evil. That is their sole purpose," the man answered. "The one to whom you refer as the Gatekeeper is one of the many arms of this evil. He is employed by the forces that would throw events off their intended track. If they can do so by spreading unnecessary death and destruction among humanity, so much the better."

"I knew he was bad from the start," Emma whispered.

"And you were very right, young lady," the man said. "Although I might substitute the word evil for the word bad, as they are not necessarily equal in meaning."

"Why us, though?" Marcia asked. "Why did he, this Gatekeeper person, involve us in his evil doings? I mean, we didn't know the first thing about Mary Ellen MacDonald before all of this."

"Well," the man began, "for that, we have to go back a hundred years, in what you understand as time."

"What do mean, what we understand as time?" Rob asked.

"You have a certain understanding of the concept called time. In fact, it is much more complex than you know." The man gave a little wave of his hand. "But there is nothing to be gained from delving into those complexities. For our purposes, I will try to explain things in such a way as to fit into your concept of time."

He turned his gaze upon Marcia to signal he was done with this tangent. "A century ago, the Gatekeeper's employer, for lack of a better word, saw an opportunity to spread evil through manipulating Mary Ellen MacDonald."

Emma leaned forward. "He started all the fires!" She looked from one parent to another. "I saw him do it when I was there."

The man sitting across from her made a sardonic smile. "Well, I won't say he started all the fires, but he certainly did start the most dangerous of them. In short, he took advantage of the situation to make matters worse for Mary Ellen. The Gatekeeper's job was to sow hatred between Mary Ellen and her parents."

"To the point where she'd kill them?" Marcia asked.

"Exactly to that point. You see, if Mary Ellen killed one or both of her parents, not only would it spread needless death, it would also throw events off the track of their intended end."

211

Marcia frowned. "What was the intended end?"

The man blew a stream of air through pursed lips. "The answer to that is too complex for me to even begin to convey." He rubbed his hands together. "The good news is Mary Ellen did not possess the resolve to carry out his plan, no matter how much resentment the Gatekeeper filled her with. His plan failed."

Rob anticipated the next turn of the story. "But that wasn't the end of it."

"No. As you can attest, it was not. The Gatekeeper's employer, and again, I use this term because it's familiar to you, was displeased with the failure. He sentenced the Gatekeeper to rectify his failure, regardless of how long it took him to do it. It took him a century to find you."

"But I still don't know why he chose us," Marcia said.

Her comment shifted the man in his chair. "That's difficult to explain to you. Let's just say he had to find souls that matched the MacDonald family, including a young lady with more resolve than Mary Ellen."

Rob put up his hands to pause the narration. "But we're nothing like the MacDonalds. I don't see how we could possibly be a match for them."

"In terms of outward appearance, you are quite correct," the man agreed. "But on a different level, you are a remarkable match for the MacDonalds. One might even say you are a once-in-a-hundred-years match. I don't expect you to understand, but finding you was a great stroke of fortune for the Gatekeeper. Except for one thing." He gazed at the baby, sleeping in his car seat. "You were about to become the wrong-sized family. He's a handsome lad, by the way. Baby Charlie, I believe. Congratulations."

The parents each mouthed a silent thank you.

"I think the Gatekeeper would have preferred to let Emma grow a little older before he used her in his plans," the man continued.

"But the arrival of a second child would ruin everything for him, so he was forced to act sooner than he wished."

Marcia clamped a hand to her cheek. "I can't even think about him doing something to the baby!"

"He couldn't," the man quickly answered. "He doesn't have the power to seriously harm people directly. He works by convincing people to harm other people. There was no chance of the Gatekeeper convincing anyone to harm your baby. He would not hesitate to threaten the baby, of course, but he could not actually hurt him."

"Thank God!" Marcia breathed.

"Indeed," the man agreed.

Rob perked up. "So this Gatekeeper guy finds us after all these years. Somehow, we fit the mold, so he decides to use us to go back and take a second whack at getting Mary Ellen to kill her parents?"

"In a word, yes."

Before the man could expound, Marcia cut in. "Is this something Emma should be hearing?"

The man smiled. "Hear it? She lived it."

Emma put her hand on her mother's arm. "Mommy, I want to know everything."

The man nodded at Marcia. "She's already proved she can handle it, and it will help her to move on. Just like you, she seeks some measure of closure."

"Okay. Maybe you're right," Marcia said. "The thing that bothers her most, bothers us all, really, is that after all this, it seems like Mary Ellen was still left with a miserable existence."

"Indeed. I expect that would trouble you. You are remarkably compassionate people. I commend you for that. But you see, it was never a question of turning Mary Ellen's life into a happy one. There was never any chance of that."

"Why not?" Emma asked. "Why couldn't Mary Ellen ever be happy?"

The man leaned forward and spoke softly to her. "Because, as much as we would all have liked her to be happy, it was not meant to be that way. Remember when I told you not all sadness is bad? Mary Ellen's sadness served a good purpose, and it had to be that way."

Emma knit her brow and gave the man a stern look. "How could all that sadness be good?"

The man gave her an understanding smile. "Sadness can be good because there is no happiness without it. If all people knew were happiness, they'd have nothing to compare it to, and they wouldn't ever really know how precious it was."

He glanced at the parents. "Let me put it to you this way: if the world were made of gold, how valuable would gold be? Gold is valuable because of all the earth that is not gold, and happiness is precious for all feelings that are not happy."

He returned his focus to Emma. "But you should never forget, dear Emma, that because of you, Mary Ellen's life was no sadder than it needed to be, which it certainly would have been if you had not been such a good friend to her."

"Did you hear that?" Rob asked Emma. "You helped Mary Ellen a lot."

"Yeah," Emma replied. "But I still wish she could have been happier."

"We all do, sweetie," Marcia told her.

The man leaned forward and spread out his palms as if to guide his words to all of them. "The burdens of this world are not shared equally—nor can they be. It should ease your minds to understand that what you see here in your world is only the tiniest bit of the spark of life. In this world, Mary Ellen's hardships are long over and done with. But the spark of her life is not. It lives on in a different place. The soul that was Mary Ellen MacDonald has risen above that earthly suffering. I think I can assure you"—he focused his gaze upon Emma—"Mary Ellen's troubles are long past, and she is perfectly happy now."

Emma's face brightened. "Do you promise?"

The man smiled. "I do indeed."

Emma looked up at Marcia. "Mommy, I feel better now."

Marcia kissed the top of Emma's head. "I'm so glad."

"I hope my explanations have made you all feel better," the man said. "I thought I might be more helpful to you than a visit with Dr. Klavass, though I understand he is an excellent psychologist."

Rob made a pensive face. "About that. This isn't Dr. Klavass' office?"

"On the contrary," the man answered. "This is indeed his office, but he doesn't seem to be using it this week. He's on vacation, I believe, so I thought maybe he wouldn't mind us borrowing it for such an important meeting."

"How did we get an appointment, if he was going on vacation?"

The man grinned. "There are certain tricks to my trade that I'd rather not divulge. But I should tell you, Dr. Klavass has no record of you. If you still wish to speak to him, you should treat your request as if it is your first contact with his office. It might save you some awkwardness" He paused to let his words sink in. "But, I believe Emma needs Dr. Klavass not one bit more than does any other normal, happy child with loving parents."

"You think she'll be all right?" Rob asked.

"I'm confident of it. She's an exceptionally strong child. She's already proved that. She demonstrated a remarkable willingness for self-sacrifice. That takes an incredible amount of strength in any person, let alone a child. Not one in a million children her age is that strong. She will be perfectly fine."

Marcia let out a sudden and audible sob. Every eye turned toward her as she quickly wiped her eyes. "I'm sorry," she said softly.

"Don't be sorry," the man told her. "There is yet something that troubles you. Yes?"

"Yes," she replied. "You brought back that image of how it all ended. It was Mary Ellen with the gun in her hand, but I know it was really Emma making the decisions for her." She breathed several quick breaths as she searched for her words. "I just can't get it out of my head. That image. That picture of my little girl trying to commit. . ."

The man waited until he was satisfied she would not go on. "You were perhaps thinking of the word *suicide*?"

She gave him a tearful nod.

"I see." He shook his head the slightest bit. "That is quite an error on my part. I do heartily apologize. I should have seen the potential for such a misunderstanding. We must address this at once."

Marica sniffled and stared at him.

"Imagine a soldier," he began, "who throws himself on a live bomb to save his fellow soldiers. Does he do this because life has lost its value to him? Unlikely. Far more likely, he does this because life has supreme value to him, and he sees the chance to preserve many lives at the cost of only one life. Is this an act of suicide? No. This is the spirit of self-sacrifice. This is not despair; this is love."

The man turned to Emma. "Emma are you happy with your life and your family and everything?"

"Yes," Emma answered. "Especially since we got Baby Charlie. I didn't used to think I could love a brother as much as a sister, but now I think I love him even more."

The man smiled at her and turned back to Marica. "There is a quote from an old book: 'Greater love hath no man than this . . .'" He stopped, searched the space before him, and scratched his head. "This is frightfully embarrassing, but I can't remember the rest just now."

Marcia gave him a little smile through her wet eyes. "I know the rest."

"Good. I hope you will take comfort in it. It is as far as you can get from suicide."

Marcia straightened herself. "It helps, but I wish Mr. Whidden, or you, if that's who it really was, could have hit her with that door without her having to point the gun at herself."

"It all happened very quickly," the man answered. "Perhaps you had too little time to take note: Mr. Whidden, who, at my inspiration, swung the door open, could not have hit her arm under any other circumstances. If, for example, she had pointed the pistol at one of the MacDonalds, with her arm extended away from the door, there is no chance the door would have touched it. The result would have been a tragedy. Only by turning the weapon upon herself, thus extending her elbow toward the door, could the swinging door have altered the shot." He nodded his satisfaction with the outcome. "I could make Whidden open the door at that precise moment, but I could not make Mary Ellen hold her arm in the necessary attitude. That was all Emma's doing. Thankfully, she is too strong and too selfless to carry out such evil as the Gatekeeper pressed her to do. Does it make better sense to you now?"

Marica sighed. "Better. I don't know that any of this will ever make complete sense to me. But your explanation takes some weight off my mind."

"There should never be a weight on your mind when it comes to Emma. I predict your burdens will be fewer because of her."

The man let silence reign for a moment. Then he leaned forward. "Have we dispensed with this misapprehension that has troubled you?"

Marcia nodded. "Yes. I think so."

"Excellent. Then I have just a few final questions. His eyes met Emma's. "Emma, dear child, have you any fear of the Gatekeeper?"

Emma shook her head. "No. I'm too strong for him."

"Indeed. The Gatekeeper wished to find an exceptionally strong child. I think you taught him to be careful of what he wished for. Do you still worry about Mary Ellen?"

"Not anymore. Now I know her sadness is all over."

217

"Is there anything else about your travels to the other place that troubles you?"

She shook her head again. "No. It was all just a bad dream, but it's all over now."

"That's a good way to think of it." The man smiled a satisfied smile. "Well then, I guess we've accomplished everything you came here for." He winked. "And at a bargain price at that."

He rose from his chair and began toward the side door by which he had entered. "I bid you farewell," he said as he walked. "You will not be troubled by the Gatekeeper, or by myself, again."

Putting his hand on the doorknob, he told them, "You may exit by the same route you came in. Just make sure to close the outer door firmly behind you, if you don't mind; we don't want to cause any trouble for Dr. Klavass. I'm proud to have known each of you. Godspeed to you all."

He gave them a slight bow, pulled open the door, walked through, and closed it behind him.

The family on the couch watched the door for a moment longer, unsure if that were truly the end of it. At last, Emma spoke up. "Well, I guess everything's all right now that Mary Ellen is okay."

Her mother hugged her. "I guess so. How do you feel?"

"Good."

"I'm so happy to hear that," Marcia said. "Now let's go home."

They all rose. Rob picked up the car seat and followed them into the waiting room. They exited into the office building hallway. Rob was careful to pull the outer door closed behind him until the latch clicked. As soon as he'd done this, his attention was drawn back toward the door by a change beyond it. The opaque glass window in the door changed from bright to dark, as if all the lights in the office had been turned off. On the glass of the door was posted a sign explaining that the office would be closed for the entire week.

Rob pointed out the sign to Marcia. "Look at this. I didn't see this on the way in. I'd swear it wasn't there."

Marcia gave him a sly smile. "Of course it was there. Didn't you hear? Dr. Klavass has been on vacation all week."

Rob smirked. "Well, maybe he's got the right idea. What do you say we take a little vacation ourselves?"

Marcia nodded. "That's not such a bad idea. What do you think, Emma?"

Emma took each parent by the hand. "Only if we go someplace warm."

THE END